Uma & Imp

Larisa Villar Hauser

www.impprintbooks.com

UMA & IMP

Published in Great Britain by ImpPrint Books
www.impprintbooks.com

ISBN 978-0-9930361-0-1

Typeset by Amanda Ashton in Minion 12pt
Cover design by Amanda Ashton
www.AshtonDesigns.co.uk
Cover illustration by Mimi Alves

Printed and bound in England by
Clays Ltd, St Ives plc

A CIP catalogue record for this book
is available from the British Library.

For Lara,
All the way to infinity and back

Thank yous

This book would only have got half-finished if it weren't for the incredible and openhearted support of family, friends and fellow members of SCBWI (Society of Children's Book Writers and Illustrators).

There have been many times where I have been close to throwing in the memory stick and giving up. My extended A-team have pulled me back from the abyss and helped keep me going. So thank you Alex, Chrysa, Klarke, Lou, Franzi, Pollyanna and Chief Cheerleaders Victor, Greg and Ludovica.

The manuscript for this story has been through what must be a Guinness Book number of revisions. Through this process, I have had the help of numerous readers – adults, kids, professionals, writers and non-writers. In particular, I would like to thank Hero Murphy, Luke McNeil and Peggy DeAngelis' 2012 class at Jordan/Jackson School for giving me the hope that kids might actually enjoy reading UMA & IMP. Also Victor Villar Hauser, Greg Murphy, Miriam Craig, Tania Tay, Lorraine Gregory, Katy Walker, Louise Cliffe-Minns and Sue Moore-Shaw for giving invaluable feedback – sometimes more than once. Thank you everyone in SCBWI Muddlegraders. Many thanks to Bella Pearson, editor extraordinaire, whose gentle insight helped me take the story to the place that it was always trying to go.

Special thanks to Lara for showing such grace and maturity at living up-close-and-personal with the practical and emotional consequences of having a creatively obsessed mother.

I would also like to thank my parents: my mother, Hilda, whose love has transcended death, and my father, Victorino, for teaching me the wonders of a Don Quixote approach to life – believe in dreams and know that, after all, much of reality is perception.

Thank you all.

SHINY KNIGHT

A hand crept over the top of Uma's book. It was blue-green with three, spindly fingers and would have been scary except it was about the size of a 1p coin – and belonged to Imp.

Uma checked the bookshop to make sure no one was in earshot. "What do you want?" she said.

"Look at this!" Imp's black, messy hair popped into view. He swung his legs over the top of Uma's book and got comfortable. "Ta-da!" He pointed at something on the floor.

Uma sighed and looked down. A guidebook lay at her feet. It showed a rocky peak soaring above Inca ruins. "No. Not interested."

"Isn't that why we're here?" Imp said.

Uma turned back to the novel in her hand. She couldn't read because Imp's legs were dangling over the page. "Not today. Anyway, reading about Peru won't bring back Mum and Dad."

"But I pushed it over from the travel section!" Imp slid down the open page and landed on Uma's hand. "You must have noticed I was gone!"

Uma had been enjoying the quiet. "Yeah, I noticed." She turned her nettle-green eyes on Imp. "But you should be more careful. People freak out when they see stuff moving around on its own. You know that."

Uma slipped Imp into her jacket pocket. She liked the high-street bookshop because it was big, dark and mostly empty. No one else could actually see or hear Imp but they *could* see the things he did. Worse - they could hear Uma talking to him and that made her look like a total freak. So the bigger, darker and emptier a place was, the better.

Imp dragged himself out of Uma's pocket and scrambled down her trouser leg. "Buy it!" he said, landing on the guidebook's glossy front cover. "You've got that '*Apps for the Modern-day Psychic*' Aunt Calista gave you. Do a swap."

Aunt Calista was big on I.C.T. and a little kooky. "No." Uma reached down to grab Imp.

He swerved away and ran off. "Information is everything," he said. "At least check out the science section!"

"No!" Uma picked the guidebook up off the floor. "Come here!"

"Uh-uh!" Imp threw himself onto a display carousel and spun round. "The science section might have a book that gets you thinking about energy bending."

"Unlikely, as there's no such thing!" Uma said. Imp had gone on and on about Uma's *energy-bending gifts* ever since she was four and found him wrapped in Blankie, only a few days after Mum and Dad died in Peru. He meant things like levitating, walking through walls and mind reading. As if.

Imp had the display carousel spinning fast and Uma reached out to slow it down. The carousel slammed into her fingers. "Ouch! You're going to cause an accident – stop!"

Imp waved as he buzzed past. "Shan't!"

Uma took the guidebook and poked it into the carousel to stop the spinning.

And it did stop.

But the stand flew sideways.

Leaflets sprayed at high speed across the floor and the assistant rushed over from the tills. Uma watched Imp jump onto the back of a leaflet and surf across the carpet straight into the assistant's feet. When the young man picked up the leaflet Imp slithered to the floor and landed in a heap.

"What are you doing?" the assistant said to Uma, annoyed.

"Er," she said. "I, er …" For a fleeting moment, Uma wished Aunt Calista were there to help. Not that Aunt Calista was any good at talking sense to people.

But then a man appeared at Uma's side. He smiled gently as though about to explain everything. Uma hoped he hadn't seen her talking to the display carousel.

"Terribly sorry," the man said. "I am most awfully clumsy. Please don't trouble yourself, I'll clear up the mess."

And with that, he crouched down and began scooping up leaflets.

The assistant hesitated. He turned to look at the unmanned cash point then walked back to his post at the till.

"Thanks for helping out," Uma said squatting down. It wouldn't have been the first time Imp had got her banned from a shop.

"A pleasure, a pleasure." The man looked at Uma head on, eyes twinkling as though they shared a secret. He held out a hand. "I'm Felix Riley, by the way."

Small limbs scrambled up Uma's arm. She felt a pull on her long black hair as Imp settled on her shoulder. "Oh," Imp said, "a shiny knight come to your rescue!"

Mr Riley had gleaming shoes, a chiselled, film star face and gleaming white teeth.

Even though no one could hear Imp, Uma wished he would just be quiet. She ignored him and the slightly unnerving sheen on Mr Riley's gelled-up hair.

"Here." Mr Riley handed Uma a pile of leaflets. "I'll pick up, you stack."

Uma pulled the display carousel upright and began slotting leaflets into place. They were advertising a summer prize draw for a behind-the-scenes day at the zoo. She slipped one into her pocket and kept stacking.

Mr Riley gave Uma the last few leaflets and stood. He seemed to be wondering what to say. Then he pointed at the book clutched under Uma's arm. "You have an interest in Peru!" he said.

"Oh, well, sort of." Uma finished tidying. She didn't want to mention Mum and Dad. It only made people feel awkward.

Mr Riley rocked back and forth on his feet, and Uma wondered why he didn't just hurry off. That's what adults usually did.

"Are you planning a trip?" Mr Riley finally said. "I've been to the Inca ruins a few times," he squinted at Uma, studying her face. "Vast temples, stone cities. A magical place."

"No. I've never been," Uma said. "Maybe one day."

Imp tugged her hair. It was his signal that he wanted to go. She went to return the guidebook to its place on the shelf.

"So you must be familiar with Professor Harris' research," Mr Riley said, following behind.

Uma had done a lot of reading about Inca cities and gold-encrusted temples but she'd never heard of a Professor Harris. "No, I don't know his work."

Mr Riley's eyebrows sprang half way up to his hairline. "How extraordinary! He's the world's leading expert on Inca civilization. The key to everything connected to Izcal." Mr Riley's eyes scanned Uma's face as though he was trying to read her thoughts.

"Izcal?" Uma's voice wobbled. She'd never heard the

word, and felt like she was picking the wrong answer in a test.

"Never heard of Izcal? *Or* Professor Harris? That does surprise me." Mr Riley gave a small shrug. "Still, perhaps you just forgot." He walked away with a wave. "Tootle peep my dear!"

"Tootle peep?" Imp said. "Only Mary Poppins says 'tootle peep'!"

"Whatever." Uma picked Imp off her shoulder. "He didn't have to help, you know."

"So why did he?" Imp said. "All that gelled hair! The guy's a creep."

2

※

IN A JAM

Uma hung back behind the woman carrying a bag full of groceries. A wriggling bulge was tracing a path inside the bag and no way did Uma want to be blamed for whatever happened next.

The bulge rippled and after a few seconds Imp popped his head over the top. "Look what I found!" He grinned, holding a fat, jam doughnut in his spindly arms. It was already missing an Imp-sized mouthful.

Uma wanted to shout at him to stop but she'd only seem crazy. Already a big, barrel-shaped man on the street corner kept glancing over. Uma waited until the barrel man turned to his mobile then she pulled her face into an angry grimace and signalled at Imp to GET OUT of the bag. He nodded. Clutching the doughnut tight like a giant beach ball, he prepared to jump.

Uma raced forward. "Wait!" Imp was quite the acrobat, but from that height even he would break a leg.

The woman stopped, bag swinging against her calf. Imp teetered on the tips of his tiny toes, but the weight of the doughnut was too much. He plunged headlong to the ground.

"No!" Uma yelled.

Impatient, the woman turned round. "What is it?"

Too late, that's what it was. The doughnut landed with a soft thud. It rolled along the pavement and into the gutter with Imp holding on, legs thrashing as he shot round. "It's alright, I've got it," he shouted.

Uma tried not to stare at the runaway pastry. Hopefully the woman hadn't noticed she was a teatime treat down. "Erm, sorry, nothing," she said. "I thought you were my Aunt."

"Right. Well, shouldn't you be at school?"

"No," Uma said. "It's the summer holidays."

The woman scowled then turned away and kept walking.

Uma strode to the kerb. Why was Imp such a pest? She checked the road for bicycles and bent down to grab the doughnut.

But it was gone.

Disappeared.

She checked the length of the pavement in case it had rolled away – but nothing. Heart pumping fast, Uma checked the road. Luckily Imp and the doughnut weren't there. He was probably hiding so he could scoff without sharing.

Then Uma heard a loud, piercing caw and looked

over to see a huge crow sitting on a wall, doughnut at its side. She smiled. Imp would be seriously miffed that a crow had nabbed his snack, but serve him right.

Her smile froze.

The doughnut had legs. And a head.

Or, anyway, Imp was wedged through like a live skewer. He kicked and punched but was properly stuck. Uma shook her head. He never did learn. She lunged at the crow and shooed it away. The bird sunk its claws into the doughnut and flew off. Uma watched in horror as the crow headed into a tree with the Imp-filled doughnut. Now what? She peered up, trying to make out Imp's stick-like limbs. Yep – they were still thrashing, but he was no closer to wriggling free. *Why* did he have to do these things?

"Do you need help?" The voice was soft, with a gentle lilt that Uma recognised but couldn't quite place. Australian, maybe? She turned to see a boy of around her own age, eleven or so. He was stocky, had a mass of blond hair, tanned skin, and wore turquoise trousers and an orange T-shirt so bright it made Uma squint.

The boy was leaning against a fence, holding a pencil and small sketchpad in one hand. He pointed at the crow. "Do you need help?"

Uma looked up into the tree. Truth was, even if she *could* shoo the bird away, climbing had never been her thing.

The boy put down his sketchpad and Uma saw the hurried outline of a sullen man's half-concealed face drawn in faint pencil strokes. He looked shifty. It was a really good sketch of the barrel man who was still standing across the street.

The boy came over. "We'll need to get the crow away from er ..." he stared at the grubby, part-squashed doughnut, "your snack."

Uma dug around in her backpack and pulled out a packet of peanuts. She'd bought them as a way to keep Imp out of trouble between meals – another failed plan. "It won't be able to resist these," Uma said.

"Good idea," the boy said. "I'm Edgar, by the way."

Uma tossed the peanuts on the pavement, cooing, clucking and generally sounding like a mad bird lady. She'd make Imp pay for this.

After a few seconds the crow whooshed to the ground and began pecking at the nuts. Edgar shimmied up the tree, grabbed the doughnut and threw it down. "Here. Catch!"

Uma caught the flying ball just before it landed. Imp's legs poked stiff out of one end of the doughnut but his head had gone. She quickly split the pastry open and red goo seeped over her fingers. It wasn't blood though. Uma knew Imp's blood was blue. And there, splayed on his back, hair plastered in jam, was a grinning Imp.

"Have I died and gone to heaven?" he said, licking strawberry-flavoured gunk off his fingers.

Edgar climbed down from the tree and stared at the doughnut with a faint look of disgust. "Are you going to eat it?"

"Of course not!" Uma slammed the doughnut shut, even though she knew Edgar couldn't see Imp. She looked at the dusty, grit-covered mass in her fingers and wondered how to explain why she'd wanted to retrieve a filthy, half crushed and bird-mauled doughnut.

Edgar looked curious but didn't ask. Uma liked that.

"Anyway," he said, grabbing his bag. "Maybe see you around."

"Oh. Yeah." Uma lifted a hand and waved. "Thanks!"

As soon as Edgar disappeared round the corner, Uma pulled open the doughnut. "What were you thinking?" she hissed. "I mean it's not like we don't have food, couldn't you just wait?"

Imp slicked his hair back into a high quiff. "What's the stress?"

"You could have been killed!" Uma said. "Don't you know that crows love to eat worms?"

Imp pouted. "No need to be mean. Crows are really clever and have no problem differentiating between a worm and an evolved, sentient being." Imp used long words when he was upset.

"I looked like a nutcase cooing at that crow," Uma said.

"I'm sure." He popped a piece of cake into his mouth. "But you look more of a nutcase talking to a jam doughnut."

Uma scowled. "Well there's nobody around."

"Oh no?" Imp said. "Did you forget about Lardy over there."

11

Uma followed Imp's gaze to the street corner. Barrel Man glanced over but as soon as Uma caught his eye, he turned away and hurried off.

"Thanks for nothing!" Uma closed the doughnut around Imp and tossed it into her backpack.

For all she cared, he could eat his way out.

3

KNOCK, KNOCK,
WHO'S WHERE?

"You expect me to *stay in* when you go places?" Imp sounded as though he'd been offered slugs on toast for breakfast.

"You always get me into trouble," she said. "Anyway, Briar Cottage is your home, remember?" Years before, Uma had asked Aunt Calista for a doll's house. She'd wanted it as somewhere for Imp to live but he preferred roaming free and sleeping in Blankie. Uma had kept Briar Cottage anyway.

"Is this to do with my trip on the greetings card carousel?" Imp said.

"That and the doughnut incident." Uma had always thought having Imp was fun but lately he seemed more like an annoying baby brother. One that never grew up.

"Thanks to me you found out about that zoo-trip competition," Imp said. "And you might win!"

13

Uma glanced at the leaflet on her night table. She'd sent the form and was hoping for the best. "Yeah. And if I *do* you might even be allowed to come. If you start behaving."

Imp sighed and slouched over to Briar Cottage. "That thing is for girls," he said.

"Dolls' houses usually are, Imp."

Imp crossed his arms and legs. "Well, you can't force me to stay in, you know."

"You're five inches tall! Forcing you really isn't going to be a problem."

"What if I promise to behave?" Imp walked into the Briar Cottage living room.

Uma said nothing. She lay on the bed and flicked through Aunt Calista's cooking magazine. A photograph showed a big and smiling family sitting round a long dining table, heavy under the weight of food. Uma glanced at her lonely plate of half-eaten baked beans and potato waffles.

"You know," Imp said. "If you're bored, we could practice energy bending."

Uma threw the magazine onto the bed and jumped to her feet. "I'm going to shower and wash my hair." She slipped Imp into Briar Cottage and made for the door. He didn't complain. This was highly suspect. "What will you do while I'm gone?"

"Don't worry about me!" His face was pressed against a window, staring out. "I'll think of something to keep me amused. After all, I have a whole house to myself!"

14

Uma left the room and tiptoed along the corridor. Downstairs, the living room door was closed and draped in a black, velvet curtain. It was decorated with balls of scrunched up aluminium foil that were supposed to be stars. The curtain meant Aunt Calista was in a séance with her Psychic Group friends. Uma was bored but did NOT want to be around when they came out.

Being an electronics and computer whizz, Aunt Calista normally used a homemade digital Ouija board, but one time she had invited Uma to join a séance using a proper, wooden board. Afterwards Aunt Calista said it had been the most successful sitting ever. But that was only because Imp kept moving the glass around and tickling Uma until she finally shouted at him to stop. Since then, Aunt Calista believed Uma had particularly strong psychic connections.

As Uma made her way up the corridor, the living room door opened. Aunt Calista was seeing her friends out. Uma hid in the shadows and waited for them to leave.

Aunt Calista sighed. "Shame. I had a dream about Ilona and Peter last night and really thought they'd come today."

The smell of incense drifted through the house. So they'd been trying to contact Mum and Dad again. A familiar sadness made its home in Uma's chest.

"Maybe next time?" The voice was rough and husky. It was Aunt Calista's friend Ruth. She smoked around forty cigarettes a day and sounded like a talking seal.

"I guess," Aunt Calista said. "But I had one of my feelings about today. It's the anniversary of when her parents died, and usually Uma is full of questions. This year she's been all quiet and withdrawn. I think it would be great for her to chat to them, even if it's just to say goodbye."

"Say goodbye? Uma probably still wants to know what they were up to," Ruth said.

And she was right. More than anything, Uma wanted to know why Mum and Dad had gone. What they'd been hoping to discover in Peru. And what could be so important to make them leave their 4-year old daughter in the care of a whacky and very young aunt.

Aunt Calista wore long, dangly earrings that tinkled when she shook her head. "I wish I knew more," she said.

Ruth gave a deep, gravely cough. "Yes, that would help Uma, I'm sure. "

Aunt Calista was silent for such a long time that Uma leant forward to see if they'd gone back into the living room. Then Aunt Calista sighed. "You know how hard I tried to find out what happened …"

Ruth put a hand on Aunt Calista's shoulder. "It's natural for Uma to find her own way to cope. And she's only eleven, how could she possibly understand?"

Only eleven? Uma stood up to shake the pins and needles out of her legs. Eleven was nearly a teenager!

Uma headed to the bathroom and sat on the edge of the tub. What if Aunt Calista *had* given up too soon?

She'd always been more interested in spirits than in real life facts. Uma showered, washed and dried her hair, then pulled on her favourite leggings and T-shirt. Maybe there was no information about what happened to Mum and Dad because Aunt Calista hadn't tried to find out in a rational and sensible way.

When Uma came out of the bathroom the doorbell rang. She waited to see if Aunt Calista would answer. Loud knocking followed the ring and Uma hurried downstairs.

She pulled open the front door to find a tall, skinny courier dressed in a bright red boiler suit. He was an odd-looking man with a bulging Adam's apple planted in the middle of his thin neck, a bit like a small goat stuck half way down a boa constrictor's throat. "Package for Professor Harris," he said.

Professor Harris? Really? No way! "There's nobody here by that name," Uma said.

"Next door maybe?" The man had a thick American accent and sounded like a gangster from an old black-and-white movie.

Uma shook her head and looked at the man more closely. Everything about him ended in a peak: his cap, chin, nose, hair and even his teeth. This was the thinnest, most stick-like man Uma had ever seen.

"It's Friday night and this is my last drop-off," the courier insisted. "Don't you know anyone called Professor Harris?" He held out a parcel the size and shape of a shoebox then pushed it towards Uma. "It looks important."

"Sorry. I don't know anyone at all called Harris." Uma crossed her arms behind her back.

The man stared past Uma's head and into the hallway. "Is there anyone else I can ask? Like your aunt?"

Uma took a small step back. How did Stick Man know Uma lived with her aunt? "She's busy." Uma started to close the door.

The courier pushed his foot through the gap. "Bartholomew in?"

Uma relaxed a little. Stick Man obviously had the wrong house. "I don't know anyone called Bartholomew. Or Professor Harris."

"OK. I'll come back later. Yeah, tomorrow or something. Maybe your aunt can help me out, know what I mean?"

The man turned on his heels and crossed the street. Uma closed the door almost all the way. She peered through the slit to watch Stick step into a car that was the height and width of a tank. It had blacked-out windows and looked nothing like a courier truck. A big man sat in the driver's seat, elbow resting on the open window. It was the same barrel-shaped man Uma had seen in the street on the day of the doughnut incident, she was sure of it! His face was flat like a pizza, with a tomato nose and pepperoni eyes; he looked like someone who had been in more than one fight.

Uma went inside and climbed the stairs. What did Barrel and Stick want with Professor Harris? Why did they think Uma knew him? And who was Bartholomew?

She stopped on the stairs, thinking. And her brain started doing a kind of dot-to-dot picture. Professor Harris was an expert on Peru. Mum and Dad had died while on expedition there. Barrel and Stick somehow expected Uma to know Professor Harris ... What if Professor Harris was somehow connected to Mum and Dad's research?

Uma fizzed with excitement. Professor Harris might know what had happened to them!

Uma had to find him.

4

A FRIEND IN DEED

Uma trudged out of the dining room towards the stairs. She needed quiet – time to think and come up with a plan to find Professor Harris.

"Wait! Come here!" Aunt Calista's desperate cry came from the utility room.

Uma went to investigate, stopping short as she walked in. Aunt Calista was staring into the computer intently, fingers flying over the keyboard. She looked up with a fraught and haunted expression. "I need wire."

Uma waited.

"What I have isn't thick enough." Aunt Calista glanced up at the clock. "Steve's will be open and he's got everything. Get me some, will you? In the interests of science." Aunt Calista talked as though she was about to solve the problem of melting polar ice caps when in fact she was pointing at a contraption the size and shape of a brick.

"What's that?" Uma stared at the wires coming out of a strange-looking machine with a short and fat antenna.

"My latest invention – a 3rd-eye-phone. But it's not quite ready." Aunt Calista sounded proud. "I've used one of the first ever mobile phones. You know, like the ones you see in the old films from the 1980s. You can try it when I'm done."

Uma wasn't sure how a brick-sized mobile phone could ever be useful. "Hmmm," she said. "So what do you need?"

Aunt Calista handed Uma a short stub of thick electric wire. "This stuff. Get a couple of packs, in case. But not a word about what it's for! If this idea gets out, we won't be able to move for reporters. Oh, and pick up some bread for the compost bin!"

Only Aunt Calista could buy a composter, make friends with the worms then insist on feeding them fresh wholemeal bread.

Uma headed to her room without a word.

She walked in to find Imp outside Briar Cottage, resting in a hammock made from an old, stretched-out sock. He ignored her arrival and stared at the wall, nose in the air. But as soon as Uma pulled her jacket out of the wardrobe he whipped round so fast that he flipped out of the hammock, bounced off the chest of drawers and landed on the floor.

"I want to come!" He sprang to his feet. "Where are you going?"

"Just to the corner shop." Uma zipped her jacket

closed. "Come if you like, but just remember *I can't talk to you when other people are around* – at least not without looking crazy, so please don't witter on. Please?"

Imp scrambled up Uma's arm to sit on her shoulder. "I'll be quiet as a mouse," he said with a cheeky grin.

When they arrived, Uma stopped outside the shop and whispered into the crook of her neck. "Remember. Stay out of trouble."

Imp crossed his arms. "Yes, but promise to let me have an aniseed jellybean." Aniseed was his favourite flavour.

"OK," Uma said. She opened her backpack, slipped Imp into the main pouch and closed the bag tight.

"But why shut me in?" Imp shouted. "You're stifling my creativity!"

Well, that was the idea. Uma pushed open the door and walked through.

Steve, the shop owner, was sweeping the floor. "G'day!" he said, high-fiving Uma with a hand the size of a tennis racket. "It's a bit late for you, isn't it?"

"Aunt Calista has an emergency." Uma took the stub of wire from her pocket. "She needs some of this, a couple of packs maybe."

Steve put down the broom. "Yeah, I thought she might need more and ordered extra. What's she making this time?"

"Oh, you know, it's a secret as usual," Uma said.

Steve grinned. "I'll wait to be amazed then!" As he headed to the counter, the door at the back of the shop opened and the doughnut-day boy came in. He was wearing yellow shorts with a blue T-shirt and carrying a portfolio bag. "Oh hi," Edgar said when he saw Uma.

"You know Uma?" Steve sounded surprised. "Mate, you didn't tell me you'd made a friend. So how did you guys meet?"

Uma couldn't think of an easy way to explain, but luckily the shop phone started ringing and Steve went to answer.

Edgar took a seat behind the counter. He opened his portfolio and took out a drawing of a tropical bird that was as bright and colourful as his clothes.

"Did you do that?" Uma said, remembering his sketch from the day they'd first met.

"Yeah. It's a Rainbow Lorikeet. I like colour," Edgar said.

Uma didn't say that she'd already noticed. "So how do you know Steve?"

The boy assessed his drawing through narrowed eyes. "He's my uncle. I'm staying here while my parents tour England. I'm doing a summer art course."

Steve hadn't mentioned a nephew coming to stay.

Edgar pulled a pencil from his back pocket and began shading in the bird's beak. Uma noticed how his fingers were stubbier than the pen he was holding. He wasn't tall, but extra wide, just like Steve.

At that moment, Steve reappeared. "Anything else?" he said, handing over two packs of electrical wire.

"Yes." Uma dug in her jacket pocket for Aunt Calista's

money and her own rubble of coins. "A packet of jelly beans, please." She felt Imp wriggle with excitement.

"That'll be £2.76, then," Steve said.

Uma heard muffled grunts coming from her backpack. Imp, desperate to get stuck into the sweets, was trying to open the zip from the inside. She rattled the bag and felt him drop to the bottom.

Uma put the right money onto the counter. Then she had a thought. "Steve, do you know someone called Professor Harris?"

"No." He shook his head. "Why d'you ask?"

"He might live in the area and you know everyone."

"Wait!" Edgar was digging in his portfolio bag. "I do!" he said, pulling out a sheet of paper. Uma grabbed the sketch Edgar held out. Had she *already* found Professor Harris? This was incredible.

"At least," Edgar said, "I know someone who's looking for Professor Harris!"

Uma's teeth clenched. She turned to the sketch, which showed a man with dark, shiny hair and a confident smile. It was Mr Riley! So *Mr Riley* was actually looking for Professor Harris! But why?

"Who's he?" Steve said, leaning over to look at the picture.

"He came in a couple of days ago," Edgar said. "Asking about Professor Harris, just like Uma!"

Steve pulled a face. "Sorry. I don't remember him at all. You know how busy it gets in here."

Uma caught her breath. She and Mr Riley could find

the Professor together! "Do you know where he lives?"

"No, sorry," Edgar said.

Uma's excitement deflated. "Oh," she said, grabbing the sweets and bread from the counter. "Thanks, though."

Edgar gave a shy smile. "Sure."

"Uma," Steve said, "you always complain that your friends are away in the summer. Maybe you and Edgar could get together some time? He doesn't know anyone in London apart from his boring, old uncle!"

Uma was sure she heard a snigger coming from her backpack. "Well, yeah," she said in a vague sort of way. She hid her face behind a sheet of hair and left the shop in a hurry.

As soon as Uma stepped outside she saw a huge car with blacked-out windows on the opposite side of the street. Was it Barrel and Stick's car? It looked the same. Uma quickly skipped behind the corner and peered round to watch.

After a few seconds the car started up and headed down the street. As it drove past, Uma made out a silhouette that was neither barrel nor stick-shaped. She took a deep breath. Lucky. She wasn't being followed after all. Uma headed home chewing sweets.

"HEY!" The shout came from her backpack, loud and clear. "WHAT ABOUT MY ANISEED JELLYBEAN?"

5

GET THE PICTURE

The next morning, Uma sat slumped against the bathtub for some serious ceiling-staring. She needed to come up with a logical, step-by-step plan. By herself. Imp would only suggest energy bending and – who knows? – tell her to gaze into a crystal ball or something. He could be worse than Aunt Calista.

So … *how* to find Professor Harris? Where to start?

Barrel and Stick thought Uma, or Aunt Calista anyway, knew something. So Step One was to find out *exactly* where in Peru Mum and Dad had gone – and then see if there was a connection to Professor Harris' research. That much was logical. And maybe for this one thing Aunt Calista could help. The sound of high-pitched chanting seeped through the gaps around the door. At least it would be easy to find Aunt Calista.

Uma went into the bedroom to get the photo of Mum and Dad from her bedside table. Maybe looking at it

26

closely would somehow trigger Aunt Calista's memory. The picture was gone.

Uma crouched on her knees to check under the bed. Nothing. Then she looked in the bedside table. Nope.

Uma stood up. "Imp!" she shouted.

Imp popped his head through the plastic cover that made up one of Briar Cottage's downstairs windows. "You're back already?" He sounded innocent. This was a clear sign of guilt.

"Where's my picture of Mum and Dad?"

"Why?" He was stalling. Another clear sign of guilt.

"I need to ask Aunt Calista something."

"Why?"

"OK, I'm coming in!" Uma reached out to open the front of Briar Cottage.

"No!" Imp pushed her hand away. "It's behind the house! I set up an ice rink."

"I've told you not to do that, Imp. One day it's going to break!"

Uma moved Briar Cottage sideways and, sure enough, there was the picture of Mum and Dad.

Imp jumped onto the glass and slid from one end of the frame to the other. He finished with a practiced pirouette.

Uma took hold of the frame. "Off you get."

Imp didn't move. "But I'm getting really good!"

"It's dangerous, I've told you before." Uma lifted the picture and Imp slithered off.

"The problem with this relationship," he complained,

"is that it's not democratic."

Uma gently wiped the glass clean and turned to leave the room. "OK, Imp, whatever." As Uma stepped away, she felt a tug on the frame. A hook made out of a paper clip was gripping the edge of the wood. She turned to Imp. "Seriously? A fishing line?" Before she could unclasp the hook, Imp yanked the rod he'd made from string and an old toothbrush. The picture whipped across the room – and straight into the chest of drawers. There was a loud smash.

"No!" Uma grabbed the frame carefully by its edges and turned it round to see a lightning ray crack that split the glass into three jagged pieces.

"Oopsie," Imp said before diving into the Briar Cottage front garden.

Why couldn't Imp just listen? Uma carefully removed the three shards of glass and pulled out the picture. "I told you this would happen."

He poked his head through the roses. "Well, that could be called a self-fulfilling prophecy."

"Anyone else would apologise, Imp. It's lucky the picture's not damaged." Uma turned the photo over to check it wasn't torn. And there, in grey and white, was the answer she'd hoped to get from Aunt Calista! The words, written in pencil in a very neat hand, read 'Izcal, Peru'. She'd never thought to look on the back! And hadn't Mr Riley mentioned a place called Izcal? "This is amazing!" There was something else, a faint drawing of a sun with swirling rays snaking away from its core.

Imp crept to her side. "The Incas worshipped the sun."

"Yes." Uma ran a finger over the drawing. "I wonder who did this." She imagined her father sitting at a table, slipping the photo into an envelope and sealing it. Or maybe it had been Mum.

"Have a closer look, you might find something else," Imp said. "And you could show some appreciation for the way I created such a lucky accident. Maybe say thank you!"

"No thank you. And don't pretend you broke the frame on purpose just to help!" Uma went to leave the room. "I'll need a new one now – and it's lucky no-one got hurt!" She slammed the door on her way out.

Uma went downstairs to find Aunt Calista sitting cross-legged on top of a pile of cushions stacked on the kitchen table. She always did her chanting in front of the one east-facing window of the house, never mind that it was small and high up. Every now and then she would slip off the cushions and land with a crash on the floor. Only Aunt Calista could make meditation a contact sport.

Uma cleared her throat – it was something she'd learned from Imp who was a great throat-clearer when feeling ignored.

Aunt Calista had her eyes closed and her fingers wedged in her ears.

"OOOoooooooOOOOOOmmMMMM."

Uma didn't think this was how meditation was usually

practiced. She cleared her throat extra loud, like a cat spitting up a hairball.

Aunt Calista opened her eyes. "Hello!" She seemed surprised. As though she'd forgotten Uma even existed. "You alright?"

Aunt Calista's face was floppy and relaxed. Uma reckoned chanting switched off her brain and that sometimes it took a few minutes to reboot.

"Can I use the computer? I want to do some research for my science project."

"Isn't that a bit keen? You've got the whole summer to do homework."

"Please?" Uma said.

"OK, but I need to use it after lunch. I'm close to ironing out the last kinks on the 3rd-eye-phone." Aunt Calista shook her head. "Homework! You're a funny girl."

Uma didn't mention digital Ouija boards, high-altitude meditation, or 3rd-eye-phones. She went to the small bank of computers next to the washing machine in the utility room. The workspace was covered in piles of wires and strange-looking miniature circuit boards. Uma turned on the main computer and pulled a pad and paper out of the desk drawer.

Step Two was to find out everything possible about Izcal.

Uma's hands were damp with excitement. Everything was going according to plan.

6

NOTHING AND SOMETHING

Forty minutes later, Uma had found no mention of Izcal. Not anywhere. She'd learned that the Inca liked to eat grilled guinea pig (gross). And that they used the skulls of chiefs defeated in battle as ceremonial cups (double gross). But Izcal? Nothing. Not a wisp. It was as though the place didn't exist.

Next, Uma turned her attention to Professor Harris and came across a stack of research articles. Some mentioned the Professor alongside Mum and Dad.

This was PROOF they had worked together!

The problem was, although it was sort of what she'd been looking for, it didn't actually lead anywhere. She needed more information.

Uma scrolled through her list of search engine entries. Solar spectral lines, quantum vortex in a super fluid ... the same sentences kept coming up. She muttered the words under her breath, as though saying them out loud might somehow explain what they meant. Or better still – reveal some clue about where to find Professor Harris.

Uma stretched her arms over her head and yawned. Had she really expected a web search to conveniently give her something useful? Like the Professor's home address with a little map on how to get there? And maybe a fiver thrown in to cover the train fare and a snack? If it were that easy Barrel and Stick would already have tracked him down. Uma wondered about Mr Riley – what did he know? She was sure he could help.

By the time Aunt Calista stuck her head round the door, Uma was out of ideas. "I've made soy-mince casserole!" Aunt Calista said.

Uma got up. "I'll get the bread, shall I?"

"We don't need bread. It's got potatoes and carrots."

Yes, but this wasn't the first time Aunt Calista had made soy-mince casserole. Uma lifted the pot lid expecting the worst. And she got it. A dry film encrusted the dish and chunks of soggy carrot, potato and soy lumped together in a gloopy mess.

"Bummer," Aunt Calista said, "it's overcooked. I'll just pour a bit of water in, that should unglue it."

They carried the food to the table and sat down, but Uma wasn't in the mood for eating. "Do you know someone called Professor Harris?" she said after a while.

"I don't think so," Aunt Calista said. "Why d'you ask?"

"Nothing really. It's just that he worked with Mum

and Dad."

"Oh, right." Aunt Calista leaned forward, elbows on the table. She cradled her chin in her hands. "Did you want to talk about something?"

Uma rolled a piece of bread into a ball. "No. I just want to find out more about their trip."

"Yeah, but how?"

"Through Professor Harris." Uma had an idea. "We could go to Peru!"

"Right. You know what I'm like about flying, even if we could afford the tickets." Aunt Calista always said she'd rather bungee jump into a barrel of snakes than go up in a plane. "OK, forget about the fact I'm not happy flying. Let's say we go to Peru, what's the capital?"

"Lima."

Aunt Calista sat back in her chair and crossed her arms. "So we fly to Lima – and then what?"

It was a new idea. Uma hadn't worked out the details. "We could find Izcal. And maybe Professor Harris is there!"

"What's Izcal?"

"It's where Mum and Dad went." Uma wished she'd asked Mr Riley about the place. Was it an ancient city? Or a temple? Why was there nothing on the Internet?

"And where is it?" Aunt Calista said.

"I don't know – but people in Peru will!" There had to be a way to find Professor Harris.

Aunt Calista crossed her arms. "Uma, we can't thrash through the Peruvian jungle with a long stick, interviewing random strangers who probably don't speak English! Anyway, who is this Professor Harris guy?"

"He wrote research articles with Mum and Dad," Uma said. "I found them on the Internet." She didn't mention Barrel and Stick in case Aunt Calista freaked out.

"They wrote papers with lots of people, Uma. Why would he know more than anyone else?"

"He's the world's leading expert on Inca civilization!" Uma said. "Do you *really* not know anything? Even if it doesn't seem important."

Aunt Calista closed her eyes, took a deep breath through her nose then let the air out in a loud whoosh.

"Not really." She pointed to the sideboard. "There might be some papers in there, but – " Aunt Calista shuddered. "Have a look after supper, while I'm in the kitchen." Aunt Calista hated paperwork more than anything. She said forms made her itch, and would only look in the sideboard when she had a letter from the accountant. The rest of the time, bills, forms and bits of paper would get thrown into drawers. 'Out of sight, or I lose my mind', Aunt Calista always said.

Uma wolfed down supper, packed Aunt Calista to the kitchen and headed to the sideboard. It was covered with family photos of Mum, Dad and Uma's long dead grandparents. She picked up the photo of five-year old Aunt Calista, with her cheeky smile, eyes the same sharp green as Uma's and Mum's ... and that freshly coloured bright pink hair. It was bad luck how the dye had been permanent.

Uma opened the sideboard and started emptying out papers. Some were brown, flaking and looked like they'd been around since a whole other century. She went through every page, carefully searching for something that might help. Soon enough she was surrounded by messy piles of paper. Did Aunt Calista never throw anything away?

Then Uma found it. Camouflaged right at the bottom of the cupboard was a flat, black box. She pulled it out and examined the lid. DEEP, DARK, SECRET was printed in red letters over a black background. A secret? Uma's fingers fumbled as she quickly lifted the lid. She pulled out two sheets of paper headed '*Flight Itinerary*', an empty envelope and a couple of brochures on Peru. Was that it?

Aunt Calista popped her head around the door. "By the way, have you seen my coloured pens?"

Missing pens usually had something to do with Imp. Uma shook her head.

Aunt Calista's face paled at the sight of all the papers on the floor. "Did you find anything?"

Uma held up the chocolate box.

Aunt Calista grinned. "Oh yeah, that thing. I'd forgotten all about it!"

"Yes, but what's the deep dark secret?" Uma said.

"Oh, your mum had that when she was a teenager. I wasn't allowed anywhere near the thing! It's just an old chocolate box." Aunt Calista gave the papers on the floor a parting glare and left the room.

Disappointed, Uma examined the lid. Words and pictures had been blacked out from a text that originally read, *"Extra Deep Filling Dark Chocolate Secrets"*. Uma dropped the lid to the floor. Nothing! She'd found nothing useful at all!

She turned back to the papers in her hand. The brochures were new and unmarked so she put them aside. Chewing a strand of her long, black hair Uma stared at the itinerary. It had lots of letters and numbers, fare calculations and codes.

Then she saw the passenger list ... Professor I. Collins, Professor P. Collins AND Professor E. Harris. Here it was! Proof that the Professor had gone to Peru with Mum and Dad! Evidence that someone out there knew what had happened to them!

The question *now* was: had Professor Harris made it back?

7

IT'S IN THE CIPHER

"Tsk," was all Imp said.

At first Uma thought he was unimpressed with the gloopy soy mince casserole – and she couldn't blame him. But he took the food without saying a word and sat at the Briar Cottage dining table without even a tiny complaint. Something more serious was going on.

"What is it?" Uma said.

Imp stabbed a particularly rubbery lump of soy, twizzled it in front of his face and ate.

"What's wrong?" she tried.

"Nothing at all." Imp crossed his legs and turned his back on Uma.

She sat on the floor in front of the house. "Please don't be angry. I have some incredible news!"

Imp peered at her as though she was something large and sticky he'd found in a crumpled tissue. "Yes, it's always about you, isn't it? Really Uma, you must try to be less self-absorbed!"

Then she noticed.

Oh no.

"What have you done?"

Imp jumped up. "I've been working on it for days! Good, isn't it?"

Every single one of Briar Cottage's first floor internal walls had gone and been replaced by – nothing. "The house will collapse!"

Imp shook his head and pointed. He'd taped coloured pens along the walls and ceiling.

"Aunt Calista's been looking for those pens!"

"Struts, not pens," Imp said. "I'm quite the engineer, you know!"

No wonder he'd been upset. Uma hadn't noticed his handiwork. "But why? What's the point?"

Imp ran from one end of the house to the other, turning cartwheels on the way. "It's open plan, Uma. It's what I've always wanted! And everyone has open plan these days."

Uma thought of the small kitchen, living and dining rooms downstairs. "Not everyone, Imp."

"Well, everyone with any style." Imp bounced up and down with excitement. "Go on! Admit it's brilliant!"

"Well, it's -," Uma took in the broad open space and the way Imp had created separate areas by grouping furniture around the rugs. "You know, there still seem to be different rooms even though the walls are gone," she said. "That's probably why I didn't notice straight away."

"Either that or because you've got your head in the clouds and can't even see what's in front of your eyes." Despite Imp's edgy tone, she could tell he was pleased. He did three somersaults and a backflip to end up just outside the front door.

"Well, it's not as though you're interested in *my* life," Uma said, holding out the box. "Look what I've got."

Imp lay on the couch. "No chocolate for me, thanks!"

"It's not chocolate." Uma threw the box onto her bed.

"Cookies?" Imp's nose twitched with excitement.

"No. Some papers from Mum and Dad's trip."

Imp splayed out his jacket to make a parachute, and floated off the chest of drawers onto the bed. "Let's see!"

He glanced at the brochures. "Tourist Office stuff," he said. "This kind of leaflet just gives a general impression of the country." He stabbed at the pictures. "Llamas, Inca ruins, colourfully dressed indigenous people. If you were actually going to Peru you'd need a proper guidebook, like the one in the bookshop. It's no surprise they didn't take these along."

"What about this?" Excited, Uma pointed at the itinerary. "It's PROOF that Professor Harris knew Mum and Dad AND went to Peru!"

"Hmm, Professor E. Harris." Imp said. "What do you think the E. stands for?" He turned his gaze upwards, as though he kept a list of names glued to the ceiling. "Ellison, Edmund, Eustace."

"What about plain old Edward?" Uma said. She couldn't understand why Imp always had to complicate everything.

Imp shrugged. "How does it help, anyway?"

Uma dropped the papers back into the chocolate box. "Information is everything, Imp. Isn't that what you say?" Then she had a thought and fished into the box to pull out the envelope the photograph had been sent in. "The postmark is from 20th October. That's months after Mum and Dad went missing!"

Imp jumped up and down, eyes shining, as though he'd just had a brilliant idea. "Yes, so now might be a good time to look at the picture more closely! I mean, it was sent for a reason, right? Very strange, almost incredible, that there was no message, don't you think? Look at it properly."

Uma had already spent years staring at the photograph of Mum and Dad. She didn't see how looking at it again would help.

"The back of the picture, Uma." Imp sounded like the worst kind of schoolteacher. If the Briar Cottage toilet actually worked she'd be tempted to flush him down it.

Uma sighed, turned over the photo and looked closely. There *was* something. "Look, there's a page glued here!"

"Quick!" Imp said. "Have a look what it says!"

The glue was old and Uma peeled the page away without any trouble. "It's blank. There's nothing."

"You mean, nothing as far as you can see!"

Uma picked up the page and searched for anything recognisable, a letter, a shape, or a pattern. She squinted and held the page up to the light. Breathed on it. "Do you think it's one of those you have to get wet?"

"What about looking at it with your mind's eye?" Imp said.

Uma stood up to get some water. She wasn't even going to ask what Imp meant by 'mind's eye'.

He shouted after her. "You know, if you're wrong, the page will be ruined and no use to you at all. Even your mind's eye will only see mush."

Uma stopped mid track and chewed a strand of hair. "Do you remember that spy book I got a few years ago?"

Imp yawned. "I guess."

"Fruit," Uma said. "In Peru, Professor Harris would have had easy access to fruit." She struggled to remember what types of fruit could make invisible ink.

Imp curled his legs onto the chair and got out his miniature nail file. "Are you thinking lemon?" He sounded bored.

"Everywhere has lemons, right?" Uma hurried to her desk lamp, turned it on and warmed the page by placing it a short distance from the light bulb. Slowly, like figures emerging from a mist, writing appeared on the page. This was it! A clue! "I've cracked it!"

Imp got out of the chair, crawled up Uma's arm and stared at the squiggles. "No," he said. "You've revealed it – now you need to crack it!"

The page was covered in a mass of squiggles, dots

and lines. "A code!" Uma sat at her desk and examined the strange symbols. "You know," she said, "the way the writing's laid out, this could be a letter." She pointed.

"See how 'Izcal, Saturday June 21' is set on the top right hand side of the page." She pointed at three indecipherable words at the bottom, "and this is like a signature."

Uma pulled out a notebook. "I can do this," she muttered. "If we assume Professor Harris's name is at the bottom of the letter, and use Izcal, Saturday June 21, then we have a key to deciphering the letter! And look," Uma picked up the envelope and pointed at the first line of the label addressed to Aunt Calista. Then she pointed at the first set of squiggles. "This must say 'Dear Miss Howard.'" Howard was Aunt Calista's surname.

Imp sniffed in disgust. "I suppose you could do it that way," he said. "If you've got time on your hands. But it would be much quicker to just read between the lines."

That sounded about as whacky as using her mind's eye. "Let's not go there, Imp."

Uma rested her head on the desk, and spent ninety minutes matching letters with symbols. Once she'd finished she sat back, face flushed. "This is what I've got: 'Dear Miss Howard, as you may know, I was travelling with Ilona and Peter in Peru. I will soon be admitted to Parkside Hospital, Wimbledon, and need to speak to you asap. Please contact me there. Ilona asked me to help find Bartholomew. Uma may be in danger. Sincerely, Edmund Harris.'"

Imp landed on Uma's desk and scrutinized the letter. "In danger?" he said. "Cool."

"The letter's almost seven years old," Uma reminded him. "Weird though. I mean, what danger could a *four*-year-old be in?"

Imp looked Uma up and down in a way that suggested she was beyond anything as exciting as danger. "I can't imagine," he said. "Bartholomew sounds intriguing. Maybe we'll find him too."

Uma gripped the letter in her fingers. This was what she'd been hoping to find. "The main thing is, Professor Harris has information about Mum and Dad – and now I know where to find him."

"Yes." Imp raised an eyebrow. "And his name's Edmund. So I was right again!" He lay on the desk and closed his eyes. "Of course, he won't be at Parkside now though, will he?"

"Would it kill you to be encouraging?" Uma said.

"I'm just giving you a reality check!"

"You're the size of my palm, Imp." Uma rolled her eyes. "You believe in 'energy bending', have green skin and want to give ME a reality check!"

Imp recoiled. "My skin is turquoise, not green, thank you very much!" He launched off the desk onto Uma's bed and wrapped himself in the ragged, grey muslin cloth that was Blankie. "Next time you want help," he said, "ask someone else."

At that moment, the doorbell rang in loud, pulsating trills that were followed by banging. Uma jumped.

Before she could reach her bedroom door the racket stopped.

"It's for you!" Aunt Calista shouted from the hallway.

Uma rushed into the corridor. Had Barrel and Stick come back? As she reached the top of the stairs a heavy weight slammed into her chest and she rolled back onto the floor.

"Sorry!" the voice said. It was Edgar.

Uma sat onto her elbows, gasping for breath. "What's the matter?"

Edgar grabbed Uma's hand and pulled her up. "You know that man you were asking after? With the shiny hair? Well - I know where he lives!"

8

WINDOW OF OPPORTUNITY

U ma followed Edgar's bobbing red T-shirt as he ran, leading the way.

"It's really close by," he said. "I've been looking out ever since you asked about him, 'cos it seemed important, you know, to do with your parents."

So Edgar knew about Mum and Dad. Uma was glad she wouldn't have to explain. She ran, pulling her bag onto her shoulder. After a struggle and the promise of jellybeans, Imp had agreed to stay in Briar Cottage. "Thanks," Uma panted. She told Edgar about how she'd met Mr Riley at the bookshop – and her hope of finding Professor Harris.

"Who knows what Mr Riley can tell me about the Professor and Izcal," she said. "Maybe he even knew Mum and Dad!"

Edgar stopped running. "Look! It's that house there.

It's the ground floor flat. I saw him go in and everything."

As they walked slowly up to the gate Uma felt her hands break out in sweat – and it wasn't from running. What if Mr Riley knew *all about* Mum and Dad's trip? Even why they didn't make it back? Her fingers shook as she pressed the bell. The ringing echoed through the hallway and Uma waited for the sound of movement and approaching footsteps. But there was only silence. She rang again. They waited. Nothing.

"Riley must have gone out again," Edgar said. He stepped into the front garden and peered through a crack in the closed curtain. "Can't see much. Just a computer, a bunch of papers ..."

Uma led the way back down the front path. "Let's wait." There was a small park and playground on the opposite side of the street with benches set in a circle at the edges of a lawn. "We can keep an eye on the house until he gets back. If you've got time anyway."

Edgar followed her into the park and they sat down. "I've got time *and* provisions." He grinned, pulling an unopened pack of jellybeans out of his pocket.

"Mmmm, yummy ... " The voice floated up from Uma's pocket. She felt her face flush even though Edgar couldn't hear Imp.

Uma stood up. "Erm, I didn't know this park even existed," she muttered trying to sound really interested. "Will you stay here while I have a look around?"

Edgar popped a couple of jellybeans into his mouth. "Sure." He held the pack out to Uma. "Have some."

"Yes, do!" Imp said.

Uma dug into the packet and pulled out two aniseed beans and a few other flavoured sweets. "Thanks." She walked across the playground and hid behind a jungle gym. "How did you get out?" Uma pulled Imp out of her pocket. "You know I didn't want you here!"

Imp looked shocked. "But I can help."

Uma scowled. "You're staying in my backpack. Out of trouble!"

Imp pulled a full-on pout with bulging lips and droopy eyes. "It's not fair. Why should you and *PicassOz* have all the fun?"

"*PicassOz*?" Uma said. "Really?"

Imp crossed his arms and stared at the floor. "So how many jellybeans do you have?"

Uma checked her hand. "Five."

Imp turned his eyes upwards. "I calculate it takes me about six minutes to get through one jellybean. You know, if I reeeeaaaally take it slow. So five jellybeans will keep me busy for half an hour. Is that long enough?"

"But I don't even know when Mr Riley will show up!" Uma said.

"Hmmm." Imp scowled. "Guess you're going to need some more *provisions* then," he said, imitating Edgar's Australian lilt.

Uma sighed. "OK." She was just slipping her bag off her shoulder when Edgar came running round the corner.

"He's back!" Edgar said. "Come on, he's here!"

47

Uma dumped Imp into her pocket and raced behind Edgar. When they reached the street, she saw Mr Riley step out of a car, slam the door closed and head up the path to his house.

Uma stopped running. "Oh no," she said.

"Oh no," Imp said.

But Edgar was already half way across the road. She hadn't told him about Barrel and Stick or their black, 4-wheel drive. The same black 4-wheel drive Mr Riley had just stepped out of.

"Edgar, wait!" Uma shouted, but not too loud. No way did she want to be heard. "Wait!" she hissed.

"It's going to take more than that!" Imp lifted himself half way out of Uma's pocket, one arm high over his head. "Here, watch this beanball." As he flung a hand forward, Uma realised what he was doing. Too late. A red jellybean flew across the street and landed with a thwack on the side of Edgar's head. A second projectile swiftly followed and whacked his cheek. Edgar turned towards Uma, one hand covering his face.

Uma mouthed a 'sorry' and waved him over. Edgar scooted back across the street. Just as Imp was about to launch another missile, Uma grabbed his arm and pressed it into his waist. She flitted into the park and hid behind a bush. "Stop it!" she said. "That's enough."

"Mission accomplished though. PicassOz has been demobilized," Imp said. "See how I help?"

"Thank you." Uma didn't sound even a little grateful. "But I need you to stop now."

Edgar's blond head appeared round the bush. "What are you doing?" A red fleck throbbed on his cheek like premature acne.

"Oops," Imp said, "guess I have a pretty strong pitch,"

Uma stuffed Imp into her pocket and turned to Edgar. "Sorry about that."

He looked confused. "Isn't that Mr Riley?"

Uma explained about Barrel and Stick. "I should have mentioned before."

A crease appeared between Edgar's eyebrows. "Yeah," he said. "So Mr Riley is friendly with a couple of crooks!" He peeked around the bush towards the house. "The car's still there, engine running. Shall we wait?"

Uma ignored his question. Even though Imp had thought Mr Riley was a creep, she couldn't quite see him in cahoots with criminals. He didn't seem the type. "Do you think Barrel and Stick have somehow fooled Mr Riley into helping them? Or something?"

Edgar peered round the corner into the street. "Well," he said, "there's one way to find out. Riley just got in the car and they've driven off." He reached in his pocket and pulled out a red Swiss Army knife. "This could help. Let's see what we can find out."

Uma wasn't sure. "Break in?" she said. "What if they come back? Or what if someone calls the police?"

Edgar led the way. "We won't break in," he said, "but maybe he's left a window open or something."

"Look!" Uma pointed. "There's a path at the side of the house Maybe there's a window round there."

Uma led the way past a line of bins.

"Oh yeah!" Edgar pointed at a small window that was tipped open and held in place by a lever.

"We can't get through there," Uma said.

Edgar cupped his hands and peered through the big, closed pane of glass. "No. You'd have to be tiny."

As though on cue, Imp jumped out of Uma's pocket, scrambled up the frame and through the top window.

"No!" Uma said.

"What?" Edgar pulled away from the glass. "I didn't do anything."

"Erm, sorry, I ..." There was no way to explain. But she needed to sort Imp out. "I just thought that it's probably best to double check there's nobody in. I mean, we weren't watching the car the whole time."

"Fair point. I'll go ring the bell again." Edgar made his way to the front of the house.

As soon as he was out of sight, Uma climbed onto the wide ledge and pulled her face up to the crack of the open pane. Lucky Mr Riley didn't believe in window boxes. "Imp!" she hissed. "Get out of there now!" She peered through the glass. "Where are you? What are you doing?"

The sound of the doorbell rang through the house. Uma saw Imp struggling to crawl up the inside of the window. He had a large piece of chocolate tucked under one arm.

Uma pushed a hand through the gap but couldn't reach. "Put that down and get OUT of there!" she said.

Leaning his back against the window surround, Imp clung onto the handle with his free arm and pushed with his legs. The lever moved open and he splat-landed on the carpet.

Edgar re-appeared at Uma's side. "I thought you didn't want to break in!"

"What?" Uma jumped back. The window was wide open. "Oh, I er, I just rested my hand on the pane and the whole thing sort of swung open." Uma looked into the room but couldn't see Imp anywhere. "Is this illegal? Like breaking and entering?"

"No," Edgar said, "because we didn't break anything and we don't need to enter. Look!"

With the window open they had a clear view of the room. A massive whiteboard hung on a wall. It was covered in black writing and there was a central bubble with the word 'Harris' written in the middle. Arrows shot out to other bubbles with a series of different words: 'Izcal', 'Uma', 'Calista', 'universities', 'hospitals', 'Bartholomew' ... Bartholomew again!

"Your Mr Riley's pretty serious about finding Professor Harris, isn't he?" Edgar said. "And who's Bartholomew?"

"I don't know. Barrel and Stick asked about him too. And he was in the coded letter." Uma took in the room with its small sofa, armchair and coffee table. Every surface was covered in papers and files.

Edgar wriggled onto the window ledge and stretched as far as he could into the room. He grabbed a bunch of papers from a pile. "They're photocopies of newspaper clippings," he said.

Uma felt a tug at her side and looked down. Imp was climbing into her jacket looking happy. His face was smeared with a glistening, dark substance and he clutched two squares of chocolate against his chest. At least he was safe.

Uma took the papers.

Edgar looked over her shoulder and pointed at two words: El Jefe. "That means The Boss in Spanish," he said.

A headline read 'El Jefe returns'. Uma tried saying the words. "El J-" She hesitated.

"The 'j' is pronounced a bit like an 'h'. Like El Hefe. That's what my Spanish teacher says."

"Listen to this," Uma said. "'Patients and staff at a Chicago clinic faced a night of terror when a man known as El Jefe took over a hospital room and interrogated its occupant. The patient is in a critical condition and unable to help police with their enquiries. This is the twelfth such incident over a period of five years and security services are at a loss to understand the purpose of the attacks.' Do you think Mr Riley is trying to find El Jefe?"

Edgar grabbed another piece of paper. "Here. Check this out."

As Uma took the page she caught sight of Imp running across the living room floor towards the hallway. He was probably on his way back to the kitchen. She sighed and turned her attention to the sheet of paper. "It's a list of patient details at a Chicago clinic."

"And here." Edgar thrust another page into Uma's hand. It showed a grainy CCTV picture of three men, one big and heavy, another slight and stick-like. The third man was of average height and build, with hair gelled flat onto his head. A caption read '*CCTV images of the Chicago Crew*'.

"Oh no. I can't believe it," Uma stared into the room. "Mr Riley and El Jefe are the same person! He's a criminal who's spent years trying to track down Professor Harris. But why?" She looked back at the photograph and read the rest of the caption. "'*The man in the centre is a pharmacologist*.'" She checked the picture. "Stick is a pharmacologist? Why do they need medicines?"

"'They each have a role." Edgar leaned over Uma's shoulder and pointed at the men in turn. "El Jefe is Master Mind, Barrel is Master Muscle and Stick is Master Medic."

Uma wriggled onto the ledge and reached in for more papers. Before she could get any, Edgar grabbed the back of her jacket and yanked her to the ground. "I heard something!" he said.

Uma rubbed her grazed tummy. It was probably Imp rifling through kitchen cupboards. "I'll look." She slowly stood and peeked into the room. Sure enough, Imp was scurrying across the living room clutching a red-wrapped mini Kit Kat. His black eyes were panic-filled and small beads of orange sweat dotted his forehead.

The living room door flung wide open and Mr Riley,

or El Jefe, walked in, mobile phone cradled against his ear. He was carrying another box.

Uma ducked. Well, that explained Imp's terror. Edgar gave Uma a questioning glare and she nodded.

El Jefe's gruff voice trailed through the open window. "I just arrived with the last box of papers." He paused, listening to the person on the other line. "Yeah, we're getting closer. I just need a little more cash to keep me going."

Uma couldn't believe the strong American accent. So the whole Mr Riley, British gentleman thing really had been a total act!

"Come on," El Jefe continued, "when have I ever let you down? You'll get your money back!" He paused again. "It's big. Huge. Why else would I have spent all this time lookin'? This gig is gonna make more money than you can even imagine. But listen, I gotta go. Just wire the money and I'll call you later."

Uma heard the clutter of El Jefe's mobile as it hit the coffee table.

"What the heck?" El Jefe said. Then the window slammed shut.

Uma and Edgar shrank against the house wall and waited. With the window closed it was difficult to hear what El Jefe was doing. After a few minutes, Edgar pointed to the street. Uma shook her head. Imp wasn't out yet; she couldn't leave.

Slowly, Uma peered over the ledge. But with the window closed, she couldn't see into the room.

A red ball flashed past her face and hit the ground with a thud. Imp lay spread-eagled on the ground, Kit Kat at his side.

Uma slumped next to Edgar. "OK. Let's go," she whispered, quickly flinging Imp into her pocket.

Edgar nodded. "Weird the way that chocolate came out of nowhere. Could be drugged." He picked the Kit Kat off the ground and threw it into a bin on his way past.

Imp climbed up Uma's arm and settled onto her shoulder. "What did he do that for?" he said sulkily.

Uma's green eyes flashed at Imp. Her expression was grim, disappointed and more than a little peeved.

"Well," Imp said, "while you and PicassOz were skulking, I found out some very important information."

9

TINY TERRIFIED

The next morning Uma woke early and bright. Today was the day she would find Professor Harris – and hear all about Mum and Dad's trip. Her hands and face burned with excitement, and a touch of fear.

Imp's big discovery was that he'd spotted Parkside Hospital on El Jefe's whiteboard. He said it had been way down the list, but even a small possibility of bumping into the Chicago Crew was terrifying.

Briar Cottage was quiet, and Uma crept to her bedroom door. She was SO not bringing Imp along, not after he'd raided El Jefe's kitchen.

Uma rushed to the bathroom, got dressed and went downstairs for breakfast. She'd arranged for Edgar to come to the house, and the plan was to head for Parkside as soon as he arrived.

Aunt Calista's voice wafted down from the landing.

"I've got to run! I'm teaching class in forty minutes! There's a veggie hotpot in the oven for lunch so please don't touch anything."

Humming to herself, Uma made two pieces of toast with butter and honey.

Aunt Calista appeared in the doorway wearing her all-white yoga kit. "Wow, what's going on with you?" She waved a hand in Uma's general direction. "Your aura's glowing bright pink. Not sure I've ever seen it *that* colour before! What are you up to this morning?"

Uma put down her toast, feeling guilty. She hadn't actually told Aunt Calista about the coded letter or anything else. "Nothing," Uma mumbled through a mouthful of toast. "Edgar and I might go to the library for a bit, that's all."

"Oh, sorry, I forgot to tell you. Edgar put a note through the door to say he can't make it today."

Uma's mood deflated like a whoopee cushion. What could be more important than coming to Parkside Hospital?

"Anyway, I've put the laundry on," Aunt Calista said, heading for the door, "including some of the clothes off your bedroom floor and that old Blankie of yours."

"Blankie!" NO. Uma jumped to her feet in full emergency overdrive. She ran to the utility room. "You've turned it on!"

"Of course. Come on Uma, it's gross. Sometimes that thing needs a wash!"

Uma pushed her nose against the glass door. "Is it a

boil wash?" She caught sight of Imp's head tumble past, water swishing round his ears.

"No, but what does it matter? Seriously, you think *I'm* strange! Anyway, I need to go." Uma watched as Aunt Calista lifted the lid of the composter and cooed at the worms. "Bye, bye my dears – be good!"

Uma stood away from the washing machine. There was nothing to be done, not one thing. "Sorry!" she mouthed as Imp travelled round kicking the door on his way. There'd be hell to pay that was for sure. Imp had a mean streak and last time he'd been put through a soaking he'd poured glue into Aunt Calista's shower cap. Never mind pink hair dye; that was the day she'd discovered what having a bad hair day really meant.

"I should be back around one!" Aunt Calista rushed off with a piece of toast in her mouth. The front door slammed and Uma turned on the computer. Now Edgar wasn't coming she might as well wait for the washing machine cycle to finish.

Intending to get a head start on learning about Mum and Dad's research, Uma searched for 'superfluid, quantum vortex'.

"In a superfluid, a quantum vortex," she read under her breath, "is a hole with a superfluid circulating around the vortex axis ..." Oh boy. That didn't even make sense. She flinched as a drop of warm water sprayed into her eye.

"Talking to yourself is the first sign of madness, you know." A pale and dripping Imp stood on the desk.

"You got out!" Uma took a face towel from a pile of laundry on the floor and carefully wrapped it round Imp.

"Well observed, Einstein," Imp croaked softly. "But let me tell you, swimming through laundry-clogged water and climbing out of the soap drawer isn't easy. The only reason I managed to avoid drowning is because I've had practice. Don't you think it's strange how Aunt Calista can't follow your basic and very simple request not to put Blankie in the machine without asking?"

Usually Imp ranted after being put through the washer but his mood was strangely calm. This was a very bad sign.

"Why don't you come to Parkside Hospital with me?" Uma said. He needed a distraction to take his mind off revenge and no way could she leave Imp home unsupervised, not after a soaking.

"Well," Imp said, rubbing dry his wispy, black hair, "seeing as PicassOz let you down, it would be selfish of me to let you go alone."

They set off after getting Imp a change of clothes and soon arrived.

Parkside Hospital was a white-painted building set behind high, black gates. It had a large driveway and steps leading up to the main entrance.

"Time for you to get in my backpack," Uma said.

Imp gasped. "After everything I've been through today." His eyes welled with orange tears. This was very unsettling.

Uma slung the bag over her shoulder and climbed the steps. "One chance, Imp, just one!" She stepped through the revolving doors. "Best behaviour or you're going right into my bag."

He nodded. "Of course."

Uma stepped into a plush-carpeted reception area and stopped still. A part of her wanted to turn back. What if Professor Harris had left without trace? Then she wouldn't get to find out about Mum and Dad's trip after all. And that would be too disappointing.

"Are you planning to stand here long?" Imp said from her shoulder. "Because I didn't have breakfast and there's a snack machine over there."

"No! I'm ready." Uma walked towards a bored-looking woman behind a reception counter.

"Hello." Uma tried to sound polite and charming, "I'm looking for someone who was here about seven or eight years ago?"

The woman looked up from her computer monitor. "Patient or staff?"

"Patient," Uma said. "A Professor Harris."

The woman typed a few words and scrolled down the screen for a while. "Oh yes, Edmund Harris. Admitted in October ... yes, seven years ago."

Uma's hands gripped the counter. "I'd like to know where he went from here," she said.

The woman scanned the screen. "Discharged the following May."

"Discharged to ... ?"

"I can't tell you," the woman answered.

"Patient confidentiality," Imp said. "Obvious really." He jumped off Uma's shoulder and walked along the top of the reception desk to where a tall vase of flowers stood.

Uma wasn't ready to give up. "I need to find the Professor because he knows what happened to my Mum and Dad," she pleaded. "They died when I was four and he's my only way to find out anything about them."

The woman's eyes narrowed. "Are you making that up?"

Uma shook her head.

"Sorry, there's no information." The woman sat back and crossed her arms.

"You are actually right," Imp said, "energy bending isn't the only way!" He wedged his back against the vase and pushed. It fell over the receptionist's desk, spilling rank water everywhere. The woman jumped up and grabbed papers off her desk. Imp gave Uma a quick thumbs up and grin.

Uma couldn't believe what he'd done. "I'm so sorry," she said to the woman. "Can I help?"

The woman had found an old tea towel and was mopping up water. "It's not your fault," she said, "don't worry." She was too busy to notice her computer mouse move mysteriously across its pad.

Imp looked up at Uma. "There's nothing," he said. "No information on where Professor Harris went."

Uma scowled at Imp.

The woman dropped into her chair. "Look," she said, "First floor, left of Hubert Wing, there's a small office. Try Mr Wilkins. He might remember something. Professor Harris was here for a long time and if anyone knows anything it'll be him. Though I should warn you, he's been in a really weird mood today."

"Thank you, thank you so much!" Uma said. She wiped a strand of soggy, brown leaf from her finger and headed for the lift.

"She should have been clearer," Imp said with a sniff. "I was trying to help."

Uma said nothing until the lift door closed. "Clearer?" she said. "Her exact words were: 'Sorry, there's no information'!"

The lift opened onto the first floor and Uma stepped into the corridor. "Just don't cause trouble while I talk to Mr Wilkins. This is really important."

Uma found the right room and peered through the square glass window in the middle of the office door. A small man with thick curly hair sat behind an enormous desk scribbling notes into a file. Uma knocked gently and the man jumped back as though he'd been kicked by a donkey.

"The nervous type," Imp said from her shoulder.

"Come in!" He had a breathy, trembling voice.

Uma held a finger over her mouth and gave Imp a glare. She pushed open the door and walked in.

Mr Wilkins stood behind his desk clutching files against his chest like a shield. His shoulders dropped when he saw Uma, and he gave a small smile. "It's only you," he said. Then, perhaps realising he wasn't making sense, sat down and started again. "I m-mean, good morning. How can I help you, young lady?"

Uma stepped further into the room. "I've come to ask if you remember a Professor Harris who was here between October and May seven years ago."

Mr Wilkins writhed as though he'd just plunged a finger into the electric socket. "What is this? What do you mean? I t-told you everything I know. You promised to leave me alone if I told you!" Mr Wilkins rubbed his arms and Uma noticed a ring of red welts round his thin wrists.

Imp sucked in his breath. "Oooh, that looks like something more serious than eczema."

Uma thought the marks looked a lot like the rope burns she got in gym class. "Who promised?" she said, even though it could only be the Chicago Crew.

Mr Wilkins cowered in his chair as though he wanted to slip right through and disappear. "A nasty man with gelled-up hair. He came with a big, round guy and his skinny friend."

"Look, I'm nothing to do with them," Uma said. "Do I look scary and mean?"

Imp chuckled. "You can be!"

Uma started to pull her bag off her back and the chuckling stopped.

Mr Wilkins slumped forward. "Sorry, I'm being silly. Haven't been myself," he said. "You're just a child." He nodded, as though trying to reassure himself he was safe.

"When were they here?" Uma said.

"Not here!" His voice rose into a squeak. "At home, early this morning." Mr Wilkins sobbed. "They've been looking for the Professor for years. Said they weren't going to let one small weak man stand in their way." This sounded like a direct quote.

"Did you tell them where he is?" Uma said.

Mr Wilkins hid his face and nodded. "They made me tell, under pain of ..." his voice faded into a frantic whisper, "under pain of pain."

Uma felt desperate but couldn't think of a way to convince Mr Wilkins. "*Please,*" she said, standing up, "tell me where to go."

"But I can't!" Mr Wilkins' face wobbled with dread. "One of them said he's a pharmacologist. That he could kill me off and no one would know what happened."

"You have to tell me!" Uma couldn't believe this small, fearful man was the only thing stopping her from finding Professor Harris.

"Odd chap; scared of his own shadow," Imp said. "Shall I push one of these books to the floor and really make him jump? Maybe we can scare him into telling us."

Mr Wilkins walked over to the office door and pulled it open. "Leave now, or I'll call security."

Uma walked stiffly into the corridor. Before Mr Wilkins could close the door she spun back. "If they find

Professor Harris before I do, then whatever happens to him will be *your* fault!"

Mr Wilkins' eyes widened but his face set hard. "It's for your own good, little girl. There's nothing you can do to help, believe me, these men are dangerous." And with those words, he closed the door in Uma's face.

10

HELP?

Uma and Imp left the building.

"Out of all the hospitals on the list, they had to try Parkside first?" Uma couldn't believe the bad luck.

"Probably because it's closest to you," Imp said.

"I guess." Uma plodded down the quiet street. How was she ever going to find Professor Harris now? "Let's go to Steve's," she said. "Maybe Edgar will be back."

Imp crawled from Uma's shoulder, down her arm and into her pocket. "Don't forget PicassOz let you down today. And I risked my life coming with you! We could easily have run into the Chicago Crew."

"Right," Uma said. "As though you'd rather have stayed in!"

When they arrived at the shop Steve was pulling on his rugby shirt. "Hello mate," he said. "What's up? You're looking a bit glum!"

"Oh, it's nothing."

He pointed at her face. "Nothing doesn't look like that! Nothing's blanker, you know, flat-faced. Best thing when you're feeling like that," Steve squished his lips into a tight, sad grimace, "is to stop worrying."

Uma thought for a second. She had no clue how to find Professor Harris even though he was in serious danger. And she had a definite suspicion that she was in over her head. Was that the same as worrying? It felt more like frustration, disappointment and fear, all rolled into one. She needed help. "Is Edgar here?"

"He's been out all morning," Steve said. "Actually, I thought he was with you."

Weird. Where did Edgar go?

Steve tapped numbers into a calculator. "So how's your aunt doing?"

Imp gave a snort from deep inside Uma's pocket. "Oh, the crazy lady's just fine!"

Uma guessed he was still upset about the wash cycle. She looked at Steve and pulled a face. "Busy with her invention." She twirled a strand of hair between her fingers. "You know what she's like. Not ordinary."

"That's alright," Steve said. "Ordinary is boring!" He looked over Uma's shoulder and pointed towards the window. "And speaking of the devilish!"

Uma turned to see Aunt Calista's face pressed flat against the glass.

Rushing out from behind the counter, Steve swung open the door. Aunt Calista tumbled through, straight into his chest. Bouncing upright she brushed down her clothes. "You're open! I thought you might have left for rugby already."

"Always here for you!" Steve didn't mention that he'd just closed up the till, and Aunt Calista walked deeper into the shop.

"Great." Imp popped his head out of Uma's pocket. "The loon's arrived."

Aunt Calista grinned when she noticed Uma. "Hello! This is perfect timing! We can go home together. And I have good news!" Aunt Calista dug into her bag and pulled out a bright yellow piece of paper. "YOU WON a trip to the zoo! Can you *believe*?"

Uma tried to look happy. "Oh, great." She'd never won anything before but getting up close and personal with zoo animals didn't seem exciting. Not when Professor Harris was in danger.

Aunt Calista put the letter back in her bag. "Have a look when we get home," she said. "I need to sort out lunch!"

Steve's smile was wide and warm. "What can I get you today?"

Aunt Calista blushed, as though the pink from her hair was reflecting over her face. "Something simple, I thought. Maybe oven chips," she paused. "Not oven, no. No. Perhaps something I can boil? In a bag? Rice!" She seemed relieved. "Yes, rice and …"

Steve took Aunt Calista by the elbow and steered her to a shelf. "Sometimes there are recipe ideas on the back of the box. Or what about chicken and rice?" he said.

A giggle came from the dried goods aisle, and Steve chuckled.

Imp jumped out of Uma's pocket and ran up to her shoulder. "Are they flirting again?" He sounded indignant.

They peered to where Aunt Calista and Steve leaned together studying packets of rice. "Course not," Uma said.

After a while, Aunt Calista and Steve made their way to where Uma was waiting – and now Aunt Calista was grinning. "Risotto in a box!" she said. "All I have to do is add water and stir!"

Imp gave Uma's hair a gentle tug. "The perfect recipe," he said. "No actual cooking involved."

Uma pulled her hair free. It really was a good thing that nobody could hear Imp. They might not like him.

Aunt Calista put the packet on the counter. "I had that hotpot in the oven but it," she paused, "well, it didn't quite go, that is, it sort of … What's wrong with me? I can't find the right word!"

Aunt Calista fumbled in her bag for her purse. Meanwhile, Steve scribbled something on a piece of paper and held it up for Uma to read. "Not ordinary," it read, "EXTRAORDINARY!"

Uma looked at her aunt. The way her hair sprayed away from the sides of her face like an explosion. The way she'd emptied the contents of her bag and was holding them between her teeth: comb, sachet of lavender – and a pot of nail clippings. She always did her hands while driving but didn't like the mess.

Yes, Aunt Calista was extraordinary indeed.

Uma thought for a minute. Maybe the answer was to come up with an outlandish, Aunt Calista-type plan that would give Mr Wilkins a good reason to help. The only problem was: Uma didn't really *do* outlandish.

At that moment the shop door opened and Edgar walked in.

"Hi Edgar," Uma said, smiling. "Where've you been?"

He walked past as though Uma were a shadow. "I'm going to watch TV," he said to Steve before going to the door that lead upstairs.

Aunt Calista and Steve exchanged a raised-eyebrows look.

"The sensitive type," Imp said. "And so rude."

Uma watched as the door to Steve's flat closed. What was going on with Edgar?

11

ROUGH AND READY

Burnt. That was the word Aunt Calista had been looking for. The dinner was scorched and a toxic cloud of charcoal billowed through the house.

"It was really strange," Aunt Calista said. "The timer didn't ring and when I opened the oven door, that was inside!" She pointed to the sink at what looked like un-skinned, barbecued rabbit but was actually one of her fluffy bunny slippers. "When I checked, the temperature was 210 instead of 140. We may have gremlins, you know."

Uma said nothing. As soon as they'd got home, Imp had raced upstairs for '*some down time*'. Hiding, more like. She should have known there was no way he'd let the washing machine thing go.

While Aunt Calista went to make food, Uma headed to her room. On the way, she saw a note lying on the hallway table. It was the one from Edgar, typed and printed out on a computer.

Uma read it through looking for a clue as to why Edgar was so angry. But there was nothing. She folded the page and dropped it back down. Something caught her eye. On the back, right at the bottom was a line of text. It was also printed from a computer. '*3rd-eye phone sales pitch, Calista Howard*', the text read.

What? Edgar's note was printed on a piece of Aunt Calista's scrap paper!

That could *only* mean IMP had written the note. Probably because he hadn't wanted Edgar to come to Parkside. And THAT meant Edgar HAD arrived that morning – only to find the house empty because Uma had already left for Parkside *with Imp*. The little brat! Uma scrunched up the paper and stuffed it into her pocket. No wonder Edgar was upset.

Uma went into the bathroom and slumped against the tub. She had to come up with some way to find Professor Harris before El Jefe got to him. An outrageous, Aunt Calista-like plan, that would make Mr Wilkins tell her where to find Professor Harris.

But Uma's brain was an outrageous-idea-free zone. She couldn't think of one way to make the doctor *want* to help, unless it was by causing physical pain. Mr Wilkins was a scaredy-cat, but not even *he* would cave in to a threat of violence from an 11-year old girl who was a little on the scrawny side. Maybe after supper she could see Edgar and make things right. Then they could talk over what had happened at Parkside. Or what hadn't happened, more like.

"Food's up!" Aunt Calista shouted from the hallway before going back to humming and banging pots.

Uma went down and sat at the dining table. Mixed in with the smell of soot there was a faint, musty whiff of damp forest. Uma lifted the saucepan lid and sniffed. Ah yes, mushroom risotto.

"La, la, la," Aunt Calista hummed, "la, la, la," she gave a twirl and landed in her chair. "Why are you looking so glum?"

Wasn't that exactly what Steve had said? Uma looked up at Aunt Calista's flushed cheeks and sparkling eyes. "Why are *you* so jolly?"

Aunt Calista thrashed a serving spoon in the air. "Because I've done it! I've cracked the 3rd-eye phone!"

"Is it supposed to be cracked?" Uma said.

Aunt Calista dished out globulous mushroom risotto. "No! I mean it's done, it works!"

That seemed unlikely. Uma stirred gloop around her plate. "And what does it *do*?"

Aunt Calista rushed to the utility room and came back with the contraption. "It works like a Third Eye, of course! You call up and it answers all your questions. This machine is going to revolutionise people's decision-making – without them having to spend years in meditation trying to achieve higher awareness! Do you see?"

Uma didn't really.

"Oh, AND it still works as a phone," Aunt Calista said. "So nobody else will even know you're on the line to a higher power!"

Uma looked at the handset. As far as outrageous ideas went, this one was up there. "It doesn't really look like a normal phone," she said. "I mean it's a bit big."

Aunt Calista wagged her head around in a sort of yes, no nod. "It's a prototype but as the technology develops the phone will get smaller."

Uma picked mushrooms out of the rice and finished what was on her plate. "It sounds … interesting. How does it actually work?"

Aunt Calista jumped out of her chair and started clearing dishes. "That's a secret! But my starting point was the software I used for the digital Ouija board."

Uma left the table. If Aunt Calista's Ouija board was the starting point then there really was no hope.

Aunt Calista took the box-like machine and thrust it into Uma's hands. "Have a go! I need people to try it out."

Uma stared at the big grey buttons on the keypad. "Is there a particular number I should call?"

"No. Just press the call button and ask your question."

Realising she had little choice, Uma pressed the green key. The phone rang then crackled as the call connected. She wasn't sure what to say.

"Ask a question!" Aunt Calista urged.

"Er, hello?" Uma jumped at the sound of her own voice. It was deep, gravelly, like Frankenstein with strep throat. There was no reply – much to Uma's total un-surprise.

"There are still some glitches to iron out, like the voice thing," Aunt Calista said. "Go on! There must be *something* you want to ask!"

"Erm, can I do this outside?"

"Oh, a private question?" Aunt Calista said with a grin. "Sure."

Uma went into the hallway and closed the dining room door. Was it possible that Aunt Calista's outrageous idea might actually work? Well, there was no harm in trying.

Once again, Uma pressed the green button and waited for her call to connect. "Where can I find Professor Harris?" she said in a whisper that made her voice sound even freakier than before.

And in the deathly silence that followed Uma had an idea.

She glanced at the hallway clock. Seven. It might be too late. Uma quickly dialled the number for directory enquiries. Luckily the automated service was unfazed by her rasping growl voice. Once she had the number, Uma called Parkside Hospital.

"Mr Wilkins, please," she said.

"Of course, one moment." The woman on the other end of the line sounded concerned. Uma reckoned she probably thought the dodgy snarl was down to some horrific throat surgery.

Mr Wilkins' soft and hesitant voice was next on the

line. "Hello?"

Uma took a deep breath and put on her best show. "Are you having a laugh?" She drawled trying to sound American, angry and scary all at the same time.

Mr Wilkins' voice rose to a squeak. "Who is this?"

"I think you know," Uma snarled. She sounded deep, rough and terrifying. "Did you think it was clever to give my colleagues wrong information? Did you?"

"Wrong information? No, I didn't."

Uma heard a drawer open and the rustling of papers. "Fir Lodge, 74 Calonne Road, Wimbledon!" Mr Wilkins said. "That's what it says here, in black and white. I would never lie to you!"

Uma knew that much was true. "Right, well." She tried to think of a way to calm Mr Wilkins down. "Those gorillas must have got it wrong." She gave a brittle, crackling sigh. "Thanks for your help."

Uma heard Mr Wilkins drop into his chair. "Of course!" he said. "Anytime, well, I mean ..." he paused. "That's all you wanted, isn't it?"

"That's everything." Uma hung up the call.

The dining room door opened and Aunt Calista stuck her head into the hallway. "See, it works, doesn't it?"

Uma turned to Aunt Calista. "Well," she said with a smile, "sort of."

76

12

DEAD OR ALIVE

Uma quickly slammed Briar Cottage shut before Imp could slip out. "There is NO WAY you are coming with me. Not after you *totally ruined* Aunt Calista's slippers, and *faked a note* from Edgar! You are NOT to be trusted."

"And I suppose *PicassOz* will be going with you?" Imp said in a sulky voice.

"I just about managed to talk him round – no thanks to you! Anyone would think you didn't want me to have friends!" Uma headed for the door – and suddenly felt guilty. After all, she was Imp's only friend and the only person who could see him. "I'll find you something extra delicious for breakfast."

Imp didn't answer and Uma went to the kitchen. She slipped a handful of Coco Pops, a plum and two pieces of toast with an extra thick coating of jam onto a plate.

Luckily, Aunt Calista had gone out early and wasn't around to ask questions. Uma raced upstairs with the plate of food. Imp wasn't normally allowed Coco Pops because he had a way of dipping his tongue into the bowl and snuffling them up. Often as not, a stray grain would get wedged up his nose. He'd snort it out, but never into a handkerchief. Still, today Uma wasn't around to watch, and it was important to make exceptions.

"I'm back with breakfast! Coco Pops!"

Imp didn't reply. "Where are you?" She opened the front of Briar Cottage and slipped the food into the house. "Imp, where are you?"

"Leave me alone!" His unhappy voice came from one of the upstairs bedrooms.

Uma grabbed a roll of packing tape and stuck it over the Briar Cottage doors and windows.

"What are you doing?" Imp pressed his face up against the bedroom window, eyes wide with horror.

"Making double sure you can't get out." Uma headed for the door. "If you learn to behave, I'll take you with me next time."

Uma grabbed her backpack and left the house.

She'd spoken to Edgar the evening before and made up some story about getting confused by a note from a friend of Aunt Calista's, also called Edgar. Although it sounded far-fetched, Edgar had believed the story and they'd arranged to meet outside Fir Lodge. Uma had put Edgar in charge of doing a quick reccie to make sure the Chicago Crew weren't lurking around.

Calonne Road was less than a mile away and it didn't take long to arrive. A large, painted board hung outside number 74 but otherwise the property was concealed behind a high wall and an elaborate wrought iron gate.

When Mr Wilkins had said 'Fir Lodge', Uma imagined something like Briar Cottage but bigger, more sprawling. This place was even grander and wasn't a house but more of a, well, more of a lodge. Uma read the sign.

FIR LODGE
RETIREMENT HOME FOR
THE DISCERNING AND STYLISH
"Vivat donec moriamini"

"Hey!" Edgar had appeared at Uma's side. It was the first time Uma had seen him without either a sketchbook or portfolio bag. "What do you think all that means? Vivat donec moriamini?" he said.

Uma had no idea. "Looks like Italian, or something," she said. "Any sign of the Crew?"

"No." Edgar went up to the gate and peered through. "I checked all the streets round here and didn't see them, or the car, anywhere."

"Good." A buzzer with a video screen was set into the wall by the side of the gate and Uma pressed the button.

Edgar dragged her away from the intercom screen. "I don't think that's a good idea. It's better if nobody sees us, you know, so that no one can tell the Chicago Crew we were here."

The intercom crackled into life. "Hello? Hello?" a shaky voice said.

Uma didn't answer because Edgar was right.

The unsteady voice shouted out. "Pardon? Speak up!"

Uma ducked out of sight of the security camera just as the gate buzzed and slowly swung open.

"Why don't people speak up?" the confused voice muttered before cutting off.

"Let's hurry," Uma whispered.

Edgar nodded. "I reckon this is the only way in."

They ran up the long, gently curving gravel path towards the regal-looking double-door entrance. Miniature trees in pots dotted the path alongside a perfectly trimmed lawn. "Professor Harris must be loaded if he can afford to stay here," Uma said.

"Yeah, this place is like a proper English country house!" Edgar said. "Let's duck round the side and see if we can find a way in."

The main entrance swung open as they reached the top of the path. Before they had a chance to hide, a troop of chattering, giggling elderly ladies swept out and towards the gate. They bustled past a frozen Uma and Edgar.

"So much for keeping out of sight," Edgar said.

Uma pointed. "And it gets worse."

Following behind the women, a more sedate group of elderly men in trainers and loose trousers sauntered by. Uma stood aside, scanning faces as though she might somehow recognise Professor Harris even though she'd never even seen his picture. Every single one of the women and men was wearing a black armband.

"What's with the armbands?" Edgar said.

Uma knew. "It's an old-fashioned thing. People wear black armbands for mourning." She had a horrible thought. "Do you think Professor Harris died? Maybe the Chicago Crew already got to him."

Edgar didn't answer. Uma wished they hadn't waited until morning before coming to Fir Lodge. Of course the Crew would come at night – they didn't have to worry about bedtime. And they wouldn't hang about after seven years of looking!

Uma dragged Edgar through the double doors just as they were closing. She looked around the vast lobby. A winding central staircase trailed up two levels in front of roof-high windows that poured light into the bright and airy space. Bags and suitcases were piled in a corner next to the entrance. "Assuming Professor Harris *is* still alive, how'll we find him without being seen?" she said.

Before Edgar could answer they heard a voice. Uma jumped as someone touched her elbow.

"Can I help?" A tall woman with white hair that flowed down to her waist stood at Uma's side. She had a soft smile, inquisitive blue eyes and deeply creased skin.

Edgar gave a friendly smile back. "We're here to see Professor Harris."

"Is he going on a trip with everyone else?" Uma said. That would make things way more complicated but at least it would mean he was still alive.

"I'm Margaret Stanton." The woman held her hand out to the children. "People call me Maggie. I'm afraid Professor Harris won't be coming to France with us as he's had a bit of a turn."

A turn? From nowhere, Uma's eyes welled with tears. Was he *really* dead? "What happened?"

"Is he alright?" Edgar said.

Maggie bobbed her head up and down in a gentle, reflective way that Uma didn't think was a 'yes' nod. "It's a shock, I understand," the woman said. "But there's still a little time before he leaves us."

Uma held back a sob. Professor Harris wasn't dead but *dying*! What had the Chicago Crew done to him? WHY hadn't she found the coded letter sooner? He'd been living round the corner for seven years and she'd only found him when it was too late.

Maggie patted Uma's back. "Don't worry, he'll be home with you soon."

"Home?" Uma said, trying to sound innocent. That had been the plan, but how did Maggie know?

"Well, yes, home to America." Maggie put a hand over her mouth. "So sorry. I seem to be making a lot of assumptions. I thought you must be part of his long lost family."

"Oh yeah," Edgar said. "Long lost family."

Thinking quickly, Uma put on her best American accent and smiled. "I am!" she said. "He's my uncle, er, you know, once removed."

"Well, you can see him if you'd like. Just be quiet when you go up. Some of the more frail residents need their rest." Maggie smiled. "This is such a lovely turn of events. I'm sure the Professor will be right as rain soon enough. Perhaps a new family," she nodded at Uma and Edgar, "with young people, are just what he needs."

Maggie pointed upstairs. "Room 1G, first floor," she said. "Lady Montgomery, the owner, should be around if you have any questions, but I'd best get going. I don't want to miss our tour of the French vineyards! Vivat donec moriamini: live until you die! Perhaps see you when we're back in three weeks."

As Maggie pulled open the door, two men wearing yellow visibility jackets came in and carried away the suitcases.

"Awesome," Edgar said. "Everyone that's seen us will soon be out of the country!"

"Exactly." Uma dragged Edgar toward the stairs. "If we keep it that way then no one will ever know we were here!"

13

WHO'S WHO

When they reached room 1G the door was shut. Uma put her ear close up against the wood. "I can hear talking," Uma said. "Do you think the Crew are here?"

"Maybe," Edgar whispered.

Uma listened. She could definitely make out an American accent but not any words. Maggie had spoken about long-lost family in America and that was where El Jefe had been looking. So Professor Harris could be American. The voice was muttering, droning, maybe even repeating the same thing over and over ... yes, that was it, *one* voice. Uma moved away from the door. "I think he's talking to himself," she said.

"Are you *sure* though?" Edgar said. "If we run into them it'll all be over. I mean even if we manage to get Professor Harris out, they'll know to come looking at your place because they'll have seen us."

Uma listened some more. "I'm sure." She knocked on the door and edged into the room. "Professor Harris?" A man sat hunched in a big armchair facing the window. The room was light, airy, and the walls were covered in framed watercolours of delicately drawn flowers.

The Professor turned and his eyes widened in shock as he saw Uma. "It's you!" he said, in a clear American accent. Professor Harris sat forward and pushed down against the armrest as he tried to stand.

"Wow, he really *is* old!" Edgar said.

Uma thought Professor Harris was the most ancient person she'd ever seen. His shoulders drooped into his chest as though his bones were made of rubber and his skin looked thin, breakable, like moth wings. It was even the same colour as moth wings – a dusty, pale brown. She rushed to the Professor's side and helped him back into the chair. "It's OK, sit down."

He grabbed her hand and tugged, as though he'd waited a long time for Uma to arrive. "When they said my 'long-lost family', I thought HE had found me, but it's you!" He patted Uma's hand. "It's you!"

Uma sat on the footstool in front of the armchair. "You know who I am?"

Professor Harris grinned. "Well, yes, but look at you!" He waved a hand over his own trunk and face. "And look at me ... at what it did to me ... but forget all that, I have so many questions Ilona ..."

Edgar followed Uma into the room and shut the

door. "Who's Ilona?" he said.

Uma took the Professor's hand. "I'm Uma, Ilona's daughter. You sent a photograph and coded letter, do you remember?" Uma wasn't too sure that Professor Harris even remembered the trip to Peru.

"Of course you're Ilona's daughter! That makes more sense. I got stupidly confused because you have exactly her beautiful green eyes." The Professor sat forward in his chair. "Does El Jefe know about you?"

Uma nodded. "He knows where I live, but doesn't know we're here or anything."

"Ah," Professor Harris shook his head and patted her hand. "That's not good. He can't know you've found me. That man is desperate, been tracking me down for years. He's willing to do anything to get into Izcal."

Uma leaned forward. "What's Izcal?"

"The Temple of Light." Professor Harris gave a wistful smile. "El Jefe wants to get inside Izcal but he doesn't understand the danger. The power."

Edgar went to stand by the door. "We should hurry."

Uma had a million questions but knew Edgar was right. "Listen Professor, we don't have much time," she said. "El Jefe *is* the one pretending to be your long lost family and he's coming to take you away. We need to leave."

"Uma!" Edgar stood with his ear pressed up against the door. "I can hear heavy footsteps!"

Uma jumped to her feet. "We have to hide!" She looked Professor Harris in the eye. "Don't say I was here."

"Of course not." The Professor slumped into his chair and closed his eyes, pretending to sleep.

Edgar ran over to the window, pulled it open and peered out. "There's a ledge here, it's probably our safest bet, what do you think?"

As the pounding got closer, Uma scanned the room. Only someone the size of Barrel could make that much noise walking. The sound of a rumbling cough focused her mind and she ran over to the window. Edgar had already climbed out and was standing on a ledge slightly broader than the width of his feet.

"No way," Uma said. "Just, no way." She turned back into the room and threw herself under Professor Harris' bed.

"Ah, the old classic," a voice said from her pocket, "not exactly original, but it'll do."

Uma looked down at Imp's head, poking out of her jacket. She glared at him questioningly. How did he even get out?

"I did a reverse Santa." Imp looked pretty smug. "But don't worry, I'm here to *prove* that I can help."

Right. So he had got out through the chimney. Typical. Uma ignored Imp and turned to watch the door slowly open. She saw a pair of large feet stomp into the room and towards Professor Harris' chair.

Imp pointed at the thick, stockinged legs, and toes that had been squeezed into dainty, orange, open-toe ballet pumps.

They weren't Barrel's feet.

A deep, powerful but nevertheless female voice boomed out. "How are you today, Professor Harris? Quite over the delicious surprise about your family?"

"I am now, Lady Montgomery," the Professor said.

"Jolly good, jolly good. Your cousin is most terribly eager for you to join him in America," she said. "He's booked a flight for this afternoon. Isn't that marvellous?"

"This afternoon?" The Professor's voice was breathless and anxious. "Already?"

Uma watched Lady Montgomery's feet crash over to a mirrored wardrobe next to the bed. She saw her own startled face staring back from the reflection and quickly slid closer to the wall. Clothes hangers clattered onto the mattress above her head.

"Don't worry," Lady Montgomery said. "I'll pack your things, then we'll have a nice early lunch before you go. He said it was a long flight, thirteen hours."

Lady Montgomery pulled a suitcase from the top of the wardrobe. "Such a pleasant man."

"Pleasant." Professor Harris took a deep breath and began humming a strange, sad tune.

Lady Montgomery went over to the Professor. "There, there," she said. "It's a big change, but I'm sure you'll be very happy. Don't worry, nobody's taking you back to that awful place."

Uma kept her breathing shallow and silent. What awful place? Did she mean Izcal?

Lady Montgomery came up to the bed, threw down

the suitcase and began to pack. Imp pulled a grossed-out face at the line-up of toes, fat and bloated like slugs in rain. "Has no-one ever told her that rhinos shouldn't wear shoes?"

Uma shook her head. They had more important things to worry about than the size of Lady Montgomery's feet.

A sharp ring came from downstairs. "Ah! That must be him now!" Lady Montgomery scampered away to answer the door.

Uma waited until the sound of foot-thuds faded, then rolled out from under the bed. "We have to hurry!" She ran across to the window and looked out.

Imp clung onto a strand of hair and peered into the void. "PicassOz has gone!" He sounded happy.

Feeling as though she might throw up, Uma leaned out and stared down at the ground. But there was nothing. No body, no crumpled Edgar. Air steamed out of her lungs in relief. He must somehow have climbed down, though Uma couldn't see why he would do such a thing.

She turned back to Professor Harris. He was already pulling himself up onto frail, shaking legs. "All I need are my journals and papers from the bedside table." His voice was clear and determined.

Uma rushed to throw the Professor's things into her backpack. "El Jefe will come up by the stairs," she said. "Do you know of another way out?"

The Professor nodded. "This place has been my home for nearly seven years, I know my way around." He took

Uma's hand and shuffled towards the door.

Lady Montgomery's voice reverberated up the stairwell. "A nice cup of tea, my dear Anton?"

Uma tugged the Professor's hand. "Quick. Before they see us."

14

TRAPPED

Uma inched out of the room.

"Turn right, away from the main staircase," Professor Harris said.

The corridor was silent. They stayed close to the wall, away from the banister that overlooked the hall. Uma hardly dared breathe.

In the time it takes to say '*you crazy loon*', Imp strapped a rag round his head commando-style and climbed onto Uma's shoulder. "*I've got our backs!*" he said, pointing a pen as though it was a gun.

There was a sound. It was a sharp, insistent tapping. Uma saw a dark shadow in a window further up the corridor. She put a hand on Professor Harris' shoulder and pointed. The shadow swayed in the casement, rattled the frame and tapped the glass.

"Is it a ghost?" Imp said.

They stopped and stared.

Imp pointed his pen at the window. "Is it a ghoul?"

"It's your friend," Professor Harris said.

Uma ran to the window and tugged it open. A pale-faced Edgar gripped the window surround. He looked a little sick.

"Did he have to show back up?" Imp muttered.

Edgar tumbled through the open window. "It's Barrel and Stick," he said. "They're outside! I had to walk along the ledge to get out of sight and then couldn't find a way in."

Uma helped him to his feet. "El Jefe's downstairs with Lady Montgomery," she whispered. "We're trying to get out before he comes up."

"Oh," Edgar said. "I was hoping never to meet that guy. What's the plan?"

Professor Harris pointed to the end of the corridor. "See the door? It opens onto an old staircase that goes down to what used to be the servants' entrance."

"Is it near the kitchen?" Uma said. "Because that's where Lady Montgomery is."

Imp sat bolt upright. "No she isn't," he said, "they're on their way up!"

Uma dragged the Professor and Edgar by the arm. Holding a finger in front of her mouth, she pointed to the stairs. They padded silently over thick carpet and ran the last few steps to the end of the corridor.

Lady Montgomery's voice boomed up the stairwell. "You're absolutely right," she said, "I'm sure the Professor will want to see you straight away."

Uma pulled open the door and gently pushed the Professor and Edgar through. Lady Montgomery puffed her way up the last step just as Uma quietly closed the door behind herself. She was pretty sure they hadn't been seen.

Professor Harris led the way in single file down a dark and narrow bare-wood staircase. "Only a few more steps," he wheezed, "then we can get out the back."

"PROFESSOR HAAAARRIS!" Lady Montgomery's voice vibrated in a deep crescendo. "WHERE ARE YOU? YOUR COUSIN ANTON'S HERE FOR YOU!"

The Professor opened a second door at the bottom of the stairs and went through to a long, narrow room with a red tiled floor that ran from the staircase to the second, outside door.

Uma heard the sound of slamming. 'Cousin Anton' was pretty desperate to find Professor Harris. And soon.

"Let's get out of here." Edgar walked up to the heavy, wooden door, pulled the handle and gave a tug. But nothing budged. He turned the handle and pulled again. "It's locked."

"No key?" The Professor looked confused for a second. "Ah," he said, "one of the boys probably left it upstairs."

"Do you know where?" Uma said.

The Professor nodded. "Yes, inside a big vase right by the window your friend just came through."

The shouting and slamming got louder. Edgar

93

headed back to the stairs. "Does the door to this room lock from the outside?"

"Yes," the Professor said.

"Good. I'm going to lock you in and take the key. That way they'll think there's nobody here. I'll get the key for the other door then either come back, or come round from outside." Edgar closed the staircase door and left.

The key turned and Uma heard Edgar run back upstairs. "They'll see him," she said. "El Jefe's right up there with Lady Montgomery, they'll definitely see him."

"Let's hope not." Professor Harris looked around the room, saw a stool and sat down. "I guess we should wait until he's back. For now."

Uma didn't think there was a choice. She strained to hear what was going on upstairs. Had Edgar managed to hide behind the curtain before being seen? Would he be able to get back? Because how could he get downstairs and out of the front door with Barrel and Stick lurking outside? She didn't want to just sit and wait.

Imp tugged Uma's hair. "We're running out of time, Uma. You're going to have to pull your finger out and try something new."

Uma glared at Imp. What did that even *mean* exactly? This was no time for an '*energy bending*' lecture.

Professor Harris shuffled round in his chair. "Did you hear that?"

Someone was stomping down the steps towards their hideout. Uma felt like a cowering rabbit waiting for the fox's snout to appear. A heavy fist pounded the door and she jumped.

"Are you in there?" The voice was rough, angry, commanding and American. It was El Jefe. "I know you're in there!"

Imp jumped off Uma's shoulder and pelted over to the door. She reached out to stop him but he was too fast.

Lady Montgomery's rumbling tenor rang down from the top of the stairs. "My dear Anton," she said, "the Professor's probably gone for a walk in the grounds."

Imp scrambled up the door and quickly stuffed his bandana into the keyhole. Only then did Uma understand what he was doing. But it was too late.

"I saw something," El Jefe said. "I'm sure he's in there."

Uma gave Imp a grateful smile.

Lady Montgomery stomped down the stairs. "Well, if the Professor *is* in there it's probably because he's anxious about the move. I think a gentle approach might work best, don't you?"

"You're right, Lady Montgomery." El Jefe moved away from the door, his voice calm and soft. "In fact, would you mind calling in my two friends? One is a skilled er, negotiator, the other a kind of pharmacist. They could help, you know."

Negotiator? Pharmacist? Uma thought 'torturer' and 'poisoner' were better words.

"Of course!" Lady Montgomery said. "Anything to help."

Uma heard her footsteps pound upstairs. What now? She turned to Professor Harris with a questioning look.

"We need to get out of here," he said. "Now."

As soon as Lady Montgomery was out of earshot, El Jefe pounded on the door. "Open up!" he yelled.

"We can't wait for Edgar." Professor Harris pointed at the exit. "Let's just go."

Uma went over and rattled the handle. "But it's locked."

"I know," the Professor said.

Imp was perched back on Uma's shoulder. He chuckled. "The Professor knows!"

Uma clenched her fists. Being stuck in a locked utility room while being chased by a thug just wasn't funny. And why was Imp so amused? "How?" she said to Professor Harris.

A loud crash shook the staircase door. "Harris," El Jefe shouted into the keyhole. "Don't make this difficult. It'll take ten seconds to get this door down. All I need is the fire extinguisher that's in the hallway upstairs. Are you really going to make me get it? Think about it … much better you let me in. Listen, I'll give you to the count of three." El Jefe waited.

The Professor stared Uma full in the face. "You can't get through the door?" He sounded surprised, almost shocked. "It's just that your mother said …"

"Ha!" Imp laughed. "He thinks you can walk through doors!"

"What?" Uma turned to Professor Harris. "You think

I can walk through the closed door?"

"ONE!" El Jefe shouted.

The Professor looked apologetic. "Well, yes," he said. "Your mother always said you took after her, so ... yes."

What?" Uma didn't know what else to say. "My mother WHAT?!"

"TWO!" El Jefe kicked the door. "You've been hiding from me long enough!"

"She said that when you were three you could already levitate," the Professor said.

This was the kind of nonsense Imp came up with but ... Professor Harris? "You mean Mum could," she waved her hand at the door, "walk through solid objects and stuff? How? Why?"

"THREE! OK, I'm going to get that fire extinguisher. But now you've really made me mad!" El Jefe moved away from the door.

Imp tugged Uma's hair. "We're running out of time!"

The door at the top of the staircase slammed. Uma crouched next to the Professor. "Please tell me. Just quickly."

Hunching his shoulders, the Professor began. "You know your grandfather was a scientist, right?"

Uma nodded.

"Well," the Professor continued, "he died when one of his experiments ... exploded? Your mother was in the house and from then on she had these amazing abilities. You know, to work with energy in ways that the rest of us can only dream."

Footsteps crashed back downstairs. "Can I explain another time?" The Professor wiped his face with a shaking hand. "Can you at least try?"

Imp grunted like the idea was a joke.

Uma stared at the floor. It was too much to take in.

A heavy object slammed into the staircase door and Uma stood up.

"Thank you." The Professor took her hand. "Thank you."

There was another deafening slam, followed by the sound of splintering wood.

Uma felt foolish. She should have practiced like Imp said. "And I can take you through with me?" she said to the Professor.

He nodded. "It's always worked that way before."

The exit door was old, made of thick, solid wood. Uma closed her eyes and touched its cold surface.

"It's OK," Imp said. "Just try."

The loud grinding of hinges being ripped out of wood came from behind Uma's head.

She gripped Professor Harris' hand, closed her eyes and walked forward.

15

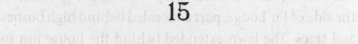

TAXI!

"See NOW what I mean by energy bending?" Imp said when they were outside.

Uma didn't react. She couldn't. Her face was frozen, her legs congealed – maybe this was what rigor mortis felt like? She reached out and pushed her hand against the wooden door. It was totally solid but somehow she'd walked straight through. AND she'd managed to bring out Professor Harris.

The Professor put a hand on her shoulder. "The boundaries between the material and nonmaterial world are less defined for you and your mother," he said. "Didn't I say you could do it?"

"As have I, many a time," Imp muttered.

A loud crash came from behind the door, followed by a monstrous roar. El Jefe had broken through and found Professor Harris not there.

Uma had so many questions but they would have to wait. She looked around. They were in the grounds at the side of Fir Lodge, part concealed behind high bushes and trees. The lawn extended behind the house just to the left. They could either sprint across in full sight of anyone who might be looking, or stay put. Professor Harris was too weak to run but staying put wasn't an option either.

Uma heard the sound of rustling leaves and breaking twigs. She grabbed the Professor's arm and pulled him behind the trunk of a wide tree.

"And it's PicassOz," Imp said with a groan.

Panting, Edgar pushed his way through a bush and into view. His trousers were dust-streaked and his face pink. "How did you get out?" he said. "Sorry to take so long but I had to wait until they were gone. Then Lady Montgomery came back and I had to hide a while longer." He doubled over and took a few ragged breaths. "Barrel and Stick are still at the front of the house, I had to come round the back. I ran as fast as I could."

"El Jefe saw Professor Harris before we er ... " Uma pointed at the door she'd just walked through. "Anyway, we should go."

There was a massive crash and the heavy wooden door trembled. "Let's get out of here."

"This way," the Professor delved deeper into the undergrowth. "There's a route that leads straight onto the street."

His voice was weak and Uma wasn't sure how far

he would get. "No need to rush," she said, following behind. Except the opposite was true. "I mean, there's no point wearing yourself out, right?"

Edgar took the Professor by the arm and helped him along.

"I'll be fine," the Professor said. Uma wasn't even a little convinced.

Imp settled into the crook of her neck. "Any chance of a jellybean? For all my hard work and helpfulness?"

Uma fished a sweet out of her pocket and slipped it into his outstretched fingers. Maybe now she could get some quiet. Time to think. Uma trailed behind Professor Harris and Edgar, trying to remember Mum ever doing anything at all energy bending-ish. She definitely couldn't remember doing stuff herself. She pulled a strand of hair into her mouth and wondered how life might be if she'd actually practiced … ? Well, practiced what exactly?

Professor Harris wiped his face with the back of a sleeve.

"Are we nearly there?" Uma whispered. She wanted to get home so Professor Harris could explain everything.

"Not too far," he answered.

Lady Montgomery's voice drifted over from the house. "I do wish you hadn't broken that door," she said. "It dates back to the 18th century. I did say Professor Harris is most likely in the grounds. Now stop fretting, he's too frail to walk far! You know, I'm beginning to wonder whether the Professor should leave with you at all."

El Jefe's reply was inaudible.

Edgar peered through the bushes. "They're coming this way," he said. "And Stick is carrying a weird-looking gun."

The Professor strode off. "We have to keep going. It won't take them long to find us."

Edgar and Uma exchanged a worried look. Before meeting Mr Wilkins and Professor Harris, Uma had never seen an adult properly scared.

They walked in silence, listening out for the sound of anyone following behind. The crunch of branches underfoot maybe, or the crash of Barrel closing in. Everything was quiet.

The Professor pointed at a row of flowering bushes that grew against a fence. "Nearly there," he said.

When they reached the bushes, he stopped, rested a hand against a tree trunk and leaned forward, breathing heavily. "There's a gap in the fence. Go ahead, I'll follow in a sec."

Uma and Edgar pulled aside branches to reveal a narrow hole that lead directly onto a quiet street. They squeezed through one at a time.

"Wait!" Imp sprang upright. "I heard something."

Uma stopped.

"What is it?" Edgar said.

"A sound," Uma said, without knowing exactly what Imp meant.

The Professor pushed half way through the hole. "Is

something wrong?"

Uma heard a strange high-pitched whistle.

"I saw something," Edgar said. "Like a small, colourful bug flying through the leaves."

The whistling sound came again. But this time it stopped abruptly like a swatted mosquito.

The Professor's head twitched.

"What is it?" Edgar said.

"I don't know," he said through gritted teeth.

"Run!" Imp yelled. "Everyone has to run!"

"Let's go!" Uma said. With Edgar's help she pulled Professor Harris through the fence. They bolted without even knowing exactly what they were running from.

Up ahead, Uma saw the high street. She looked back. The whistling had stopped and she couldn't see anyone coming up behind.

Exhausted, they reached the road.

"It's a fifteen minute walk back to the house," Uma panted.

Edgar looked doubtful. "That's quite far," he said.

Uma knew he meant it was far for Professor Harris.

Ashen, the Professor leaned forward and covered his face with a hand. "Can you find your way?"

"Of course! Let's go." Uma and Edgar turned towards the roundabout up ahead.

The Professor didn't move. "Go," he said. "If I come, I'll put you in danger."

Uma shook her head. "You have to come!"

"Where else would you go?" Edgar said.

"You need looking after." Uma wasn't going to leave Professor Harris behind. No way. "The only people who saw us at Fir Lodge are heading to France right now," she said. "El Jefe only saw you, not us."

Uma took the Professor by the arm. "They don't know you're with us, it'll be fine."

He hesitated. "Is your aunt home?"

"Yes. She loves visitors and we have a spare room," Uma said.

"I'll come, but only to meet Calista," the Professor said with a weak smile. "Let's get a cab!"

The front door flung open as soon as they got home. Aunt Calista rushed out. "Uma!" she said. "Where've you been? It's late!"

"This is Professor Harris," Uma said. "He's not very well." She was hoping Aunt Calista could persuade the Professor to stay for more than just tea.

Edgar helped the Professor up the path. Aunt Calista took Professor Harris by the elbow and led him into the house. He lifted her hand to his lips. "Enchanté Madame," he said with a gallant nod of his head.

"So you're the Professor Harris Uma has been talking about! How did she find you?" Aunt Calista said. "Welcome, come in! Would you like a cup of tea?"

Professor Harris staggered forward. "That would be great, but I just need to sit down for a sec."

Imp scrambled down Uma's arm and to the floor. "Er, Uma," he said. "I've found something."

Uma ignored Imp and helped Aunt Calista steer

Professor Harris to the living room.

She felt a tug on her arm, as Edgar pulled her back. "He's got a thing in his neck!" He pointed. "Professor Harris," he said, "in his neck."

Aunt Calista helped the Professor to the armchair.

Uma looked.

Imp was climbing up the Professor's arm and there, right in the neck, Uma saw what Edgar and Imp had already spotted. A tiny, feathered dart pierced the Professor's skin. Imp leaned forward but slipped and tumbled before he could reach.

Professor Harris lifted an arm, cried out and fell to the floor.

Aunt Calista tried to catch him, but only managed to cushion his fall. The Professor plunged face down onto the carpet.

"Uma, quick!" Aunt Calista yelled. "Call an ambulance!"

16

TRYING

Aunt Calista popped her head round the door to Uma's room. She was carrying a large volume of '*Herbology for the 22nd Century*'. "Put a saucepan of water on the boil, will you? I want to make up the Professor's morning tea."

It was the same request Uma had heard every day, a few times a day, for the last week. This wasn't how she'd imagined things would be.

The doctor had recommended bed rest because she didn't believe Professor Harris had been poisoned. Not even after seeing the feathered dart. "Home made, probably by some child playing Tarzan," she'd said.

So they were on their own. Aunt Calista had got out her book of herbs and, after hearing about the Chicago Crew, put a variety of protective crystals around the house. Apparently they would change colour at the approach of any person harbouring ill intent. Apparently. Uma had put the police on speed dial.

She was desperate for Professor Harris to feel better so she could ask about Mum and Dad. Uma dragged herself off the bed and shuffled her feet into slippers.

Imp was sitting cross-legged outside Briar Cottage. His spine was ballet-dancer straight, thumb and index finger curled into what he called a 'mood-ra'. He opened one eye to watch Aunt Calista's retreat. "Florence Nighting-fail strikes again," he said.

Actually, Uma would be glad to leave the room and get away from Imp's Tibetan Master act. Ever since the walking through walls thing, he expected her to practice energy bending ALL the time, as though rubbing it in that he'd been right all along.

Imp went into Briar Cottage and grabbed his favourite cotton scarf. "Once that brew is on, the house will be choking-full of boiled-twig smell. Let's practice in the park."

"OK." Uma went to the door. "You know, Aunt Calista says the herbs are helping," she said, even though Professor Harris had barely been upright since arriving.

Imp snorted. "G-ROSS. They smell so bad the *threat* of treatment is enough to stop anyone getting sick."

Uma opened the bedroom door. "I'll be right back."

"Opening doors is just a wasted practice opportunity!" Imp yelled.

Uma trudged downstairs. She wished Professor Harris would get better so he could explain more about energy bending and how she could be like Mum. Imp was big on bossing but thin on detail.

In the kitchen, Uma pulled out The Cauldron – anyway that was what Imp called Aunt Calista's big saucepan. She filled it with water and put it on the hob. While waiting for the water to boil, Uma put a hand on the kitchen door and pushed. But her fingers stayed fixed on the wood's surface.

Had she *imagined* the whole walking-through-wood thing? Imp said not, but her eyes had been closed, so maybe she'd missed what *actually* happened and there was another, totally ordinary and reasonable, explanation.

Once the herbs were simmering, Uma grabbed Imp and they left for the park. She settled under her favourite tree, a willow with branches that trailed almost to the ground. It made a perfect hideout where she could talk to Imp without being seen.

"So what do you prefer: Simple Levitation, Stage One Disappearing or Molecular Diffusion?" Imp paced the ground, waving his arms and ruffling his hair into a tangled mess. Uma reckoned he must have got bored with the Zen thing and moved into Mad Scientist mode. He'd been waiting years for her to listen to him about energy bending and was enjoying her attention.

"What about Disappearing?" Uma said. Molecular Diffusion was what Imp called walking through walls but neither that or levitation was working.

Imp dropped to the floor and sat in front of Uma.

"Go on then."

"Go on, what?" Uma said.

Imp waved a hand as though shooing away flies. "Disappear."

Uma closed her eyes and breathed deeply. This SO wasn't going to go well.

"It's not working," Imp said.

"Of course it's not working!" Uma said through clenched jaw. "If telling people to disappear actually made them vanish, there'd probably be nobody left on the planet. *You* wouldn't be here, *that's* for sure!"

Imp crossed his arms. "No need to get in a mood. I'm only trying to help!"

"Well maybe you could start by telling me HOW I'm supposed to disappear!"

"It should be easy. In your genes and all that." Imp stood up, grabbed a trailing strand of leaves and pulled himself up.

"Maybe I should start by making *you* disappear," Uma said.

Imp thought for a second. "OK," he said, "if it helps."

Uma rolled her eyes. "Imp, it's not that easy!"

"But look how you just walked right through that door! You just needed to try, like I always said." Imp clung onto a thin branch and swung back and forth. "Not that I'm one to say '*I told you so*'".

Uma made a choking, grunting sound. If only that were true! "Look, you must have some idea how all this works?"

Imp swung higher. "Weeeeee heeeee, this is so fun!" he yelled. "You should have a go!"

Uma watched him swing back and forth. His hair fluttered round his smiling face and the scarf trailed in the wind. He probably didn't know how energy bending worked and didn't want to admit ignorance. Why did Professor Harris have to be out for the count? He'd be able to help for sure.

"Are you in there?" A face appeared through the leafy branches. It was Edgar, portfolio hiked under his arm, dressed head to toe in white. "Aunt Calista told me where to find you."

"Oh, it's PicassOz again," Imp muttered. "Doesn't he know two and a half's a crowd?"

Uma jumped to her feet. "Is Professor Harris awake?"

Edgar pushed through the branches and into the hideout. "No," he said. "But my art teacher's sick so I've got the afternoon off."

"Tell him you're busy," Imp said. His swing got higher.

Edgar stared at the swaying branch. "Don't you think that's weird?"

"Probably just a breeze." Uma tried to think of a logical explanation for the random swaying of one solitary branch. "A localized, er, micro breeze," she said.

Edgar didn't look convinced. "Anyway, what are you doing?"

"Nothing really." Uma nodded at Edgar. "What's with the white? I thought you liked colour."

"Actually, white is all colours blended together. You

110

know, like a rainbow in hiding."

Uma remembered experiments she'd done at school using prisms. "So you must hate black."

"Not really." Edgar knelt down. "Black absorbs all light, so it's got all the colours too – just in a different way." He pulled a drawing out of his portfolio. "Look. A dart frog." It had a bright orange body, blue legs and glowing black eyes. "I looked it up. They live in South America and natives use their secretions to make poison arrows."

"Do you think that's what El Jefe used on Professor Harris?"

Edgar pulled a black pencil from his trouser pocket. "Dunno. But the arrow looks pretty native, don't you think?" He sat down and started shading black marks onto the frog's legs.

By now Imp's swinging was out of control. While Edgar was absorbed in his work, Uma pulled a face at Imp and shook her head. He took one hand off the branch and waved as he flew past.

Bad idea.

Imp launched through the air, arms splayed at his sides like a flying squirrel. He landed feet first on the dry ground and skidded straight over Edgar's picture in a flurry of dusty footprints.

"What?" Edgar looked up into the tree. "What just happened?"

Uma quickly wiped footprints off the drawing while Imp scurried into the bottom of her jacket pocket.

"Freaky," she said, standing up. "Shall we check on Professor Harris?"

17

EVEN MORE TRYING

A week later, Professor Harris was still out for the count. Worse still, Edgar had gone off with Steve for a couple of days, and that meant Uma was alone. Alone … with Imp.

"I have a plan," Imp said. He was sitting cross-legged outside Briar Cottage at the entrance to a tepee built from an old clown's hat he'd covered in a doll's poncho.

Uma lay on her bed, staring at the ceiling. She didn't react. Imp's plans never worked and usually ended in destruction.

Imp kept talking. "I've been giving it serious thought," he said, "and I've decided to be more directive."

Uma sat up. "You mean more bossy?"

"You need help." Imp poked the pile of sticks at his feet. It was a campfire, which, much to Imp's amazement, Uma had refused to light. "I've devised a way to instruct

113

you in the art of Levitation." He bounced to his feet. "What do you think? Shall we start now? I mean with PicassOz out of the way ... or, you know, *away*, we have no distractions."

Uma sat on the edge of her bed. She had nothing better to do. "OK."

Imp went into Briar Cottage and came out with one of Aunt Calista's coloured pens.

"Wasn't that holding up Briar Cottage roof or something?" Uma said.

"No. I was using this one as a fireman's pole." Imp set the pen down, moved back in front of the tepee and sat down. "So," he said, "start by staring at the pen. Really focus."

Uma sat forward and stared.

Imp jumped up. "No! Don't stare!"

"But you told me to!"

"Well I didn't mean in that *staring* kind of way!" Imp rolled his eyes as though Uma was two sugars short of a jellybean.

"What other way is there?"

Imp paced, thinking. "Gaze," he said after a few moments. "Try a soft gaze, rather than that googly, lunatic ogling."

"Right." Uma leaned forward and looked at the pencil with a soft gaze. After a while her eyes relaxed, unfocussed and dreamy. A small pellet of wet paper whacked her forehead. "Ouch!"

"No dozing!" Imp said. "You might be glad of energy

bending if ever El Jefe shows up. Stay awake! Focus!"

"Don't you think he'd already have showed up? I mean, if he knew Professor Harris was here?" Uma said.

Imp pulled his eyes wide. "Well *I* don't know how the criminal mind works." He waved his hands around. "Just concentrate."

"Doing nothing makes me tired!" Uma sat up, back straight, and tried again. Soft gaze. Focus.

"That's not bad," Imp said after a few minutes, "now imagine the pen lifting, resting on a pillow of air, light and vibrant."

Uma stared harder and tried to visualize the pen floating above the chest of drawers. She closed her eyes and imagined it flying round the room at her command.

"No!" Imp had turned from turquoise to blue – a sure sign he was losing his rag. "Don't *think*, use your ima-gi-*na*-tion!"

Imp was behaving as though he knew what was going on inside her head. "I *was* imagining," Uma said.

"You had your eyes closed, that's thinking. Now look at the pen and watch it float!"

If Imp didn't chill out, Uma thought she might also go a blue-y shade of green. She looked at the pen and tried. And tried. And stopped trying. "It's too difficult when I'm actually looking at the thing just sitting there!" she said.

Imp stared at the wall behind Uma's head. "Then spend more time focusing until the pen is light and vibrant. And don't forget you're a beginner. I'm sure your Mum had to practice."

Uma couldn't actually believe Mum had been able to levitate. Or that it was even possible. "Can I have a break?"

"Nooooo," Imp whined. "How's my plan supposed to work if you don't try? Give it another go, you're bound to have a breakthrough soon."

That seemed doubtful. Uma tried again. Soft gaze. Focus. Soft gaze, focus.

"Light, vibrant," Imp said gently.

Light, vibrant, soft gaze, light, vibrant.

Uma imagined what it would be like if the pen could float. It would be so great. She could use it to switch off the light without having to get out of bed, or … another ball of paper flipped across the room, and hit Uma straight on the nose.

"What are you doing NOW?" Imp said. He rolled another paper pellet for his stash. "If you go off into a daydream about how to use levitation for your own amusement, then of course you'll lose focus. You might as well just go to sleep!"

Uma got off the bed. She'd had enough. "Why don't *you* show me how it's done, as you're the expert?"

Imp said nothing.

Uma pulled on her trainers. "No, I didn't think so." He had such a cheek. "You don't have a clue."

"I know exactly how it works in theory! Focus, see the outcome and let it happen. But if you want to give up, like you always do, then go ahead."

Uma stared Imp down. "Right. You know *in theory*?"

Imp crossed his arms and scowled. "The point is you're the one who needs to learn, and you're just being difficult to avoid practice. None of this is about me."

Uma went to the door. "Ha!" she said.

"You'll never learn if you give up!" Imp pouted and turned his back on Uma.

A quick rap came from the door and Aunt Calista flew into the room. "Professor Harris opened his eyes!" she panted.

Uma sprang to her feet. "Can I talk to him?"

Aunt Calista's face dropped. "Well, no. He closed them again. She skipped from one foot to the other. "But it's progress!" she said. "He'll be better any day, from one moment to the next. That's how these herbs work."

Uma shrugged, hiding her disappointment. Any day seemed like a long time away.

Aunt Calista skipped to the door. "Be patient." She grinned. "It won't be long now!"

Uma followed her aunt out of the room.

"Are you going somewhere?" Aunt Calista said, noticing the trainers on Uma's feet.

"Just for a walk."

Aunt Calista looked at Uma. "With Edgar?"

"He's away." Uma gave Imp a glare. "I'm going ALONE."

18

IFB ALERT

Uma went to Steve's. The temporary shop assistant turned out to be pretty much his opposite: a woman, short, thin, very old and, well … grumpy.

"Yes?" the woman said as soon as Uma walked into the shop. "What do you want?"

"Er …" What did she want? Uma didn't know what to say. She wanted Imp to stop being a bossy know-it-all and for Professor Harris to get better. Most of all she wanted to figure out how to use energy bending – assuming it even existed. But as for why she'd come to Steve's? Well it was just to get out of the house, really.

Uma felt a grinding in her stomach. She hadn't eaten since breakfast. The grinding was followed by the realisation that she'd left her purse on the bedside table. "Steve's not here?" she mumbled, knowing very well that he was away.

"No." The woman smugly tapped a name badge made out of sticky tape and a bit of cardboard. It read *'Pamela Richards, Temporary Assistant Shop Owner'*. "I made it myself," she said, grabbing a tissue from under the counter and loudly blowing her nose. "So what can I get you?"

Instead of just leaving, Uma decided to pretend. She would act as though she didn't know her purse was at home. And when it came to paying, Pamela Richards, Assistant Shop Owner, might let her off until another time.

Uma thought for a second. She wasn't sure what she'd like to eat. Anything and quickly, was the general plan. "I'll just have a look." She darted down the biscuit aisle away from Pamela's vigilant stare.

Hobnobs, digestives, wafer biscuits, shortbread ... the choice was vast ... and easy once Uma spotted the chocolate chip cookies. Her favourite – and Imp's. Maybe a chocolate chip cookie would calm him down. He was only trying to help, albeit in his own very trying way. Uma grabbed the packet and went to the counter for what she hoped would be an Oscar-winning performance.

Giving her best sweet, and hopefully innocent, smile, she put down the packet. Pamela didn't smile back. But when she saw the biscuits her face broke into a wide grin, revealing two rows of small, pointed teeth that would have done a shark proud.

"I love those." Pamela said. "Look!" She pointed to an open pack of chocolate chip cookies behind the counter, pulled one out and chomped down. "Delicious." A flurry of crumbs sprayed over the counter.

Uma stared. Such a waste of lovely biscuit crumbs.

She took her backpack off her shoulder and started digging around. "Oh," she said after what was hopefully the right length of time. "I don't have ... hold on!" She opened the front zipper and dug around, a hint of anxious worry beginning to spread across her face. At least that was the look she was aiming for but Pamela didn't react and Uma tried harder.

"I can't find my purse!" She pulled everything out of her bag.

"Oh dear," Pamela said, still munching, and sounding completely unbothered.

Uma put everything away and held up the pack of cookies.

"Never mind." Pamela took the packet. "I'll put them back. Those shelves need a tidy anyway."

Uma watched in disbelief as Pamela carried the cookies away. She eyed the open pack behind the counter. Even though she was practically starving, Pamela couldn't find the generosity of spirit to offer her one single, solitary biscuit. Never mind let her off paying for the packet until next time. Steve wouldn't have hesitated.

"When is Steve back?" Uma said. She wished he would arrive now, before she died of malnutrition.

Pamela marched out from behind the counter and made her way to the biscuit section. "Not for a few days."

Uma gazed at the cookies. It wasn't fair. She was so starving she could even smell the biscuits' chocolatey, sweet deliciousness. Uma's mouth watered as she imagined the solid crunch of biscuit between her teeth and the way the dark chocolate chunks would melt onto her tongue. Then her jaw dropped. She squinted. No way! A small, round, cookie-like object was floating her way. Not so much a UFO as an IFB – an Identified Flying Biscuit. Her mouth shut as the biscuit wedged in her jaw. She quickly grabbed the intruder and stared at it, expecting it to speak.

It said nothing but seemed to beg to be eaten.

At least, that was how Uma interpreted the silence. She quickly checked behind her shoulder to where Pamela was absorbed in shelf rearranging. Imp had said levitation would come in handy.

Uma wolfed down the cookie.

In the interests of practice and maybe a little bit because one cookie is never quite enough, Uma had another go. After checking Pamela was still busy, she gazed at the pack of biscuits and repeated the process. The cookie floated through the air towards Uma. She grabbed it and slipped the IFB into her pocket.

"I might come back later with my purse!" Uma said. Pamela just grunted.

Once outside, Uma guzzled down the second cookie – Imp would only complain if she showed up with just one biscuit. She grinned. He had been totally wrong about how levitation worked! What was it he'd said? Focus, something and blah blah – no! It was nothing like that! Uma had it figured out. She wiped crumbs from her face. This was the breakthrough Imp had been going on about – and she'd managed it all by herself.

Mum really could bend energy; and so could she! This was the best day EVER – the beginning of a new phase. From now on, Uma would practice, practice, practice, but in her own way. Never mind Imp's theories, the cookie had levitated because she'd REALLY WANTED IT and THAT was the key …

19

GIFT HORSE

Imp was wearing his Angry hat. It was made from a snipped off end of Aunt Calista's red woolly gloves and sewn with a black and scowling, fanged mouth. The hat was hideous. And a little scary.

Uma put down her book and watched Imp clamber up the chest of drawers using the knobs as stepping-stones. He grabbed a pair of nail clippers from behind a Briar Cottage flowerpot and, without a word, began snipping off the rose heads.

"What are you doing?" Uma said.

One eyebrow arched, Imp turned to Uma. "Dead-heading the flowers. What does it look like?" He was miffed because she had worked out levitation without his help.

"Why prune plastic roses? They won't grow back." Uma was annoyed too, mostly because she hadn't managed to levitate *anything* since the cookies. Not even a pea.

Imp gave a flourish whenever a rose-head fell to the ground. "I know they won't grow back. That's the point." After a final defiant snip he tucked the nail clippers back behind the flowerpot. "I want to get some bamboo or a couple of shrubs."

Uma sat up. It had been ten days and Professor Harris still wasn't out of bed. Imp was in a mega-strop. And she wasn't sure when Edgar was back. "It's only morning," she said, "and I'm already bored."

Imp tugged Angry hat down over his ears. "Well that's because you have nothing to practice. You know, now you've mastered levitation and walking through walls." He gave a fake, choking snort of a laugh. "Or, maybe we could move onto something more difficult – like flying!"

Now Uma was interested. "Could Mum fly?"

Imp rolled his eyes. "I don't know. Did she have wings?"

Uma threw herself back on the bed. "You're so funny." She drifted into a daydream about swooping through the air, weightless but with the power of an eagle. "Seriously though," she couldn't help asking, "do you think I could learn to fly?"

Imp crossed his legs and nodded sagely. He still put on the Tibetan Master act when he was in the mood. Even though he hadn't managed to teach Uma a thing about energy bending. And even though no Tibetan

Master would ever need an Angry hat. "Well," Imp said, "all you have to do is find a way to generate aerodynamic lift, propulsive thrust, and …." He sprang to his feet, waving his hands. "Of course you can't fly! You're not a fairy, or Supergirl!"

The doorbell rang and Uma jumped off the bed. "I'll get that!" Anything was better than listening to Imp.

Uma hurried downstairs but Aunt Calista was already closing the front door. "They're outside!" she said in a hoarse whisper, back pushed up against the door.

Uma stopped still. Did Aunt Calista mean the Chicago Crew? Why would they show up now, after two weeks? "Outside?" she said. "What are we going to do?"

Aunt Calista waved a piece of paper in the air. "Get ready! Look. The driver gave me an itinerary. We totally forgot in all the excitement!"

"An itinerary?" Uma took the paper and read. '*Today's the day! Get closer to animals than you ever dreamed possible!*' It was the lucky draw! The trip to the zoo! "It's today!" Uma said.

Aunt Calista clapped her hands and hopped from one foot to the other. "A huge limousine! With a driver and everything!"

But it was Tuesday. "Aren't you working today?" Uma said. Tuesdays were Aunt Calista's busiest day.

"Oh no." Aunt Calista stopped bouncing. "Of course. I've got five yoga classes to teach, and I can't cancel at the last minute." Aunt Calista scowled. "I can't believe we forgot."

Uma looked at the bit of paper. "Can I go alone?"

"No need!" Aunt Calista grinned. "We'll ask Professor Harris."

"But he's hardly been out of bed in almost two weeks!"

"It happened just like I said." Aunt Calista grabbed Uma by the hand and dragged her into the kitchen. "Come and see!"

Professor Harris stood at the sink wearing Aunt Calista's apple-heart apron and purple rubber gloves. He was up to his elbows in foam. "Good morning!" he chirped.

"Oh, hello." Uma couldn't believe the transformation. The Professor glowed with energy and looked at least ten years younger – 92 instead of 105. "You're better," she said.

As soon as Aunt Calista had explained about the trip to the zoo, Professor Harris unknotted the apron. "Too darn right I'll accompany the young lady! I've got a serious case of cabin fever."

The doorbell rang again and Aunt Calista rushed off.

"Are you sure you're well enough?" Uma said when she and Professor Harris were alone.

"You bet. Can't guarantee I won't be dog-eared by the evening, but I wouldn't miss it for anything." He looked serious for a moment. "But I can't stay here for much longer, you know that, right? It won't take long for El Jefe to realise that I'm here."

Aunt Calista bolted into the kitchen. "Hurry up," she said. "The car is blocking the whole road!"

Uma ran up the stairs two at a time and bounded into her room. "We're going to the zoo!"

Imp was lying flat on his back staring at the ceiling. "Whoopee," he said, sitting onto his elbows. "And does that 'we' include 'me'?"

"Yes, but only if you take off the hat!"

Imp jumped to his feet and ripped off Angry hat.

Uma really hoped a day of fun would get Imp out of his mood. "Professor Harris is coming! Can you believe he's better? Come on Imp, let's go!"

Imp eyed the empty space. "Will there be snacks?" he said before jumping in.

"For good behaviour," Uma said. "But please don't witter on at me when we're around other people. Please. And let's have a day off energy bending practice."

Uma headed downstairs where Aunt Calista was holding open the front door. "Professor Harris is already in the car." She pushed a big hard block into Uma's hand. "Take this with you."

It was the 3rd-eye phone. "Really? But it's heavy, and what if it scares the animals?"

"I need you to try it out again," Aunt Calista said. "No one else has got it to work since you did, and I've given it another tweak so the husky voice thing is sorted. Please." She pushed Uma out of the door. "Actually wait, one more thing! Whatever you do, don't mention anything to Professor Harris about your Mum and Dad's trip. He's been muttering in his sleep about Izcal, sounding all stressed, and I don't want you to set him off when it's only his first day out of bed."

Uma couldn't believe what she was hearing. "But I've been waiting!"

"I know. Just wait a bit longer, until he's properly strong."

"OK," Uma agreed even though she really didn't want to. She stuffed the 3rd-eye phone into her bag and left the house.

The driver held open the car door, head deferentially bowed to the floor, face hidden by the black, shiny peak of his cap. Uma stepped into the limo. Aunt Calista was right. There would be time to speak to Professor Harris – he wasn't going anywhere.

20

IN THE MOUTH

U ma settled into the limousine's squeaky, leather seats while Professor Harris gazed out of the car window. He seemed excited and not in the least bit fragile.

"Isn't that your friend?" The Professor said.

Uma peered through the glass. "Driver, please could you open the window?"

The driver squinted into the rear view mirror. He hesitated then pressed a button for the window to come down.

Uma stuck her head out. "Edgar! We're going to the zoo for the day! Remember, the prize I told you about?"

"Oh wow!" Edgar rubbed a hand through his thick blond hair. "You're so lucky!"

Uma turned to the driver. "Excuse me," she said to the back of his head. "Could my friend come with us?

Is it possible?"

The driver stared straight ahead. "We need to leave," he said. "Sit back." Without waiting, he buzzed the window shut.

Uma barely had time to wave Edgar goodbye. "Sorry," she said, then sat back and strapped herself into a seat belt.

After a few minutes silence, Imp scurried out of her pocket and onto Professor Harris' shoulder. He blew in his ear and the Professor shuddered. "Ask him about rainforest animals!" Imp said. "That'll get him talking about Peru."

Uma glared at Imp who scooted over the seats, out of reach.

"Come on, you know you want to!" he said from the top of the driver's hat.

The Professor looked across at Uma. "Is everything alright?"

"Yes!" Uma sat back and stared out of the window. Imp soon got bored and came over. She quickly scooped him up and wrestled him into her bag.

Professor Harris looked up from a printed itinerary. "Are you sure everything's OK?"

"Uh-huh." Uma flushed and nodded, folding her hands in her lap. "What does the itinerary say?"

The Professor smiled. "That we'll have our own keeper to take us round the zoo all day, and that we'll see a three-toed sloth. Isn't that something?"

"Yes," Uma said.

"Just do it!" Imp whispered. "You might find out something about Mum and Dad."

Uma pushed the bag under the front seat. And cracked. "Professor Harris," she said, "you must know a lot about animals, what with all the travelling you've done. Did you see any three-toed sloths in Peru?"

The Professor sat back in his seat and crossed his legs. "We won't see the sloth until the end of the day, you know, it'll be a sort of grand finale. Most of the day they'll be showing us giraffes, lions and so forth. I'll bet you know more about those than I do. Africa is an amazing place you know ..."

And with that, the Professor launched into a long lecture about savannahs, wetland reserves and the price of yams.

Uma waited, watching the traffic go by. "Is the African rainforest very different from the South American one?" she said as soon as the Professor paused for breath.

"Ah!" The Professor closed his eyes and smiled rapturously. "Rainforests are magical places," he said. "In Africa you have chimpanzees, gorillas, elephants even."

"And what about in South America?"

"Look!" Professor Harris tapped the window. "We've arrived!"

Uma breathed deep. Maybe Professor Harris kept changing the subject because he really didn't want to talk about Peru. Maybe Aunt Calista was right.

The driver opened the door and Uma pulled her

backpack out from under the seat.

"Wow," Imp said, "he really knows how to ramble!"

Uma slung her bag over a shoulder and got out of the car. Or was *Imp* right? Was the Professor rambling, rather than purposely changing the subject?

Before Uma had a chance to say goodbye, the driver stepped into the limo and drove off. Strange man.

A young woman with pigtails, wearing a green shirt and shorts appeared. "Hello, welcome to London Zoo! My name's Annie. I'm a keeper here and today I'll be showing you around. Please come with me!" She ushered Uma through the Special Priority Gate.

"We really are getting the five-star treatment," Professor Harris said, following behind.

"Easy for you to say," Imp muttered. "I'm more trapped than any of the animals in this place!"

Annie led the way down a sloping path. "First of all," she said, "we're going to feed the spider monkeys." She sounded excited. "Usually visitors aren't allowed to feed the animals, so you're very lucky. But be careful, they can nip."

"Spider monkeys are pretty friendly," Professor Harris said. "If they bite, it's only because they're scared.

Uma felt Imp writhe. "Actually," he said, "I don't mind sitting this one out."

Annie stopped as the two-way radio strapped to her trouser belt hissed. She put it to her ear. "Hello?" A squeak was followed by a voice barking through loud, intermittent crackles. Uma couldn't make out a word of what was being said.

Annie's face dropped. "But they'll miss feeding the monkeys."

"Seems like there's a change of plan." Professor Harris folded the itinerary and slipped it into his trouser pocket. "Still, guess it's all an adventure."

Annie clipped the radio back on her belt and turned to Uma. "The good news is that you're going to meet the three-toed sloth earlier than planned!"

"That's great!" Uma said. The Professor was sure to talk about Peru now.

"Let's go!" Annie led the way down a track marked with a no entry sign. "You know, I've worked here for three years and no member of the public has ever had the chance to come close to such a rare animal!"

The Professor smiled gently. "We're honoured."

Before long they reached a scrubby, overgrown area with grimy black plastic bins lying on the ground. Uma saw a huge wooden crate with leaves and thin branches poking through the top end. It was strapped to the back of a long truck.

"Looks like Ginger's all packed up and ready to go." Annie sounded sad. "She's going to be missed." The zookeeper climbed up some steps and onto the truck then unclipped the bolt at the front of the crate. "Before we go in, you should know a couple of things. First of all, the crate is made of plastic-coated wood that keeps the temperature nice and warm. Like a rainforest, which is how Ginger likes it, but it's a bit clammy for us. Also, it'll be quite dark inside. So we'll wait at the entrance until our eyes adjust. After that, if you look high up into the tree-like structure you'll see Ginger. Don't worry about the bugs flying around her fur, they're just sloth moths."

"Sloth moths?" Imp said with disgust. "S-loth moths?"

The Professor looked uneasy. "You mean it's like a rainforest in there?"

Annie smiled. "Yes, but don't worry, there's only Ginger and the moths – no snakes, or spiders!" She held out her hand. "Let me help you."

Uma followed Annie and the Professor onto the truck and the zookeeper slowly opened the crate door. "Luckily sloths don't move fast so there's no chance of Ginger bolting, but let's hurry because we don't want to upset the ecological balance." Annie slipped through a small opening, grabbed Professor Harris' hand and pulled him in. Uma followed through the crack into what felt like a warm cloud of mist.

"Now let's wait a while," Annie whispered. "Oh and let's not make too much noise. Ginger gets easily unsettled."

A loud knock came from the other side of the door. "Annie?" It was a man. He sounded in a hurry. "Can you step out for a sec?"

Annie shuffled past Uma. "That would happen just as I was telling you to keep quiet! I'll be right back." She slipped out, leaving the door open a fraction.

The Professor shuffled his feet. "This is warmer than

the Peruvian rainforest but that earthy, damp smell is just the same." He tugged at the collar of his shirt. "Maybe I should pop out for a sec." Uma moved away as he pushed past. But just as the Professor reached the door it slammed shut.

"Sorry," Uma said. "They have to do that because of the ecological balance."

Imp tugged at the zip of her bag. "Yeah," he said, "and the Easter Bunny lives in a chocolate hutch."

The Professor tapped gently on the crate wall. "I can't hear Annie," he said.

Uma put her ear against the damp wall and heard the distinct, unmistakable sound of a bolt thud into place. "Annie? Hello, Annie!"

There was no reply. Nothing except the revving of an engine. Vibrations hummed through the floor and massaged the bottom of Uma's feet. What was going on? This had to be some mistake … unless … ?

21

SHIPPING OUT

Uma stood back from the door. "What now?"

For once, Imp said nothing.

In the half-light, she saw Professor Harris sitting in a corner. "Professor?" She went over, knelt on the bark-strewn floor and stared him in the face. His breathing was shallow and weak. "Are you alright?"

"If he's unconscious," Imp said, tugging Uma's hair, "can I have his lunch?"

Professor Harris lifted his head a fraction. "The three-toed sloth all packed and ready for shipping – I should have known." He shook his head gently from side to side. "He's taking us to Peru, and this time I won't come out alive."

Imp jumped up and down on her shoulder. "We're going to Izcal!"

Uma dropped down next to the Professor. "There

must be something we can do."

The Professor stared into the distance. "El Jefe's won. This was always his plan."

"But he couldn't have known you'd come here today." Uma took the Professor's hand. It was hot and clammy. Like the tropical inside of the crate. "Aunt Calista said I shouldn't talk to you about stuff because it's upsetting. Thing is, I don't know why El Jefe wants you in Peru or, well, I don't know anything."

"I'm sorry, Uma." The Professor squeezed her hand. "I don't remember the details."

"But you said going back would kill you, so you must remember something," Uma said.

The Professor shook his head. "Light," he said. "A rainbow – and a lot of golden light. Your mom's bravery. She had so much power in her hands. I really thought she could keep us safe. But I don't remember exactly what happened."

"Do you remember who Bartholomew is?"

"I know nothing about Bartholomew. It's a name your mom shouted out ... at the end. She told me to find him."

Uma wasn't sure she understood. "If you don't remember what happened, why are you so scared?"

Professor Harris took off his jacket and rummaged through the inside pocket. He pulled out a small, blue book with gold writing on the cover. "Back page, take a look." He squeezed the booklet into Uma's hand.

It was the Professor's U.S. passport. Uma turned

to the back. The photograph showed a much younger Professor Harris and Uma saw the passport had expired. "What am I looking for?" she said.

Imp dangled on the end of her hair and peered at the picture. "Oh, wow! That is freaky."

"Date of birth." The Professor pointed half way down the page.

Uma couldn't believe what she saw. "But that makes you ..."

Imp chuckled. "In desperate need of anti-wrinkle cream."

"You're about the same age as my parents!" Uma didn't know how to put it politely. "But you look way older."

The Professor gave a sad smile. "You got it," he said. "Remember when you came to Fir Lodge and I thought you were Ilona?"

Uma nodded.

"See ... " The Professor hesitated, "when I got out of Izcal I'd aged A LOT. So when I first saw you I thought the reverse must have happened to your mom, because of the energy bending and everything. You know, that she somehow got younger." He rubbed a hand through the thin strands of his hair. "It's crazy but I always wished your parents had survived, even though I know ... well, I just I know they didn't."

A rock settled in Uma's stomach. She'd always wished the same. "How can you be sure they're dead when you don't remember what happened?"

The Professor supported himself against the wall and stood up. "In the beginning I remembered more but it kind of erased over time. Some sort of coping mechanism, I guess." He paced up and down, feet crunching on bark.

Uma had so many questions. "What's in the temple that would make you age fifty years?" she said. "Even if you don't remember what happened, you must know why you all went? What you wanted to find?"

The Professor sat back down. "Now *that* I can answer," he said. "We wanted to find Lake Iticanga. The Incas believed that deep underground there was a pool of healing light. You know, scientists have studied different energy forms for years but your mom had a cutting edge, what with levitation and all the rest. Anyway, we wanted to find Iticanga and study what was there."

Healing light? That was pretty major. Uma felt a wave of relief. She'd always *known* Mum and Dad wouldn't have left for any old reason. "What about El Jefe? Where does he fit in?"

"He was head of a clinic in Peru," the Professor said. "I stayed there for a few months after I got out of Izcal. I was in a bad way, delirious and confused. He sat with me and talked to me about my night terrors. For a long while I thought he wanted to help. Then one time I came across his notes and realised he just wanted to get to Lake Iticanga, and that he was actually using drugs to keep me talking. He wants to be the only person with access to the lake's healing light, so that he can use it any way he wants. And he wants to make money." The Professor looked angry, disgusted. "El Jefe has no idea of the danger, the power! I may not remember what happened, but one thing's for sure, not even your mom made it out alive."

Uma took Professor Harris by the arm, and gently pulled him up. "Let's prepare an escape. Someone will come in with water and food, we can get out then."

"There's something else," the Professor said. "The reason El Jefe wants to find me is because he thinks I have the key to the temple. The way in. At first I was worried he knew ... that's why I wrote that letter to your aunt ... " He stared Uma intently in the eyes and gripped her arm hard. "But of course, I haven't had the key until now. Do you understand?"

The truck stopped, motor still running. Uma had a sudden idea. This was their chance. "Professor Harris! I could walk us through, like at Fir Lodge!"

The Professor nodded. "Yes, that's right."

Before Uma could do anything, the truck lurched off. It had probably stopped at a red light – and stepping off the high truck and into moving traffic would be suicide, especially with an old man in tow. There had to be a better way. She had to think. "It'll take less than an hour to get to the airport, we need a plan. Is there something I can do with energy bending?"

Uma heard a voice from high above her head. "Hmm, walking through the crate is too risky." Imp was sitting next to Ginger, gnawing on a chunk of apple. "You could try levitating a cookie."

"Do you have an idea?" Professor Harris said. "Something to do with Ginger?"

Uma scowled at Imp and turned away. "No idea," she said. It was incredible in how many different ways Imp could say 'I told you so'.

They sat in silence for a few minutes. Then Uma had a thought. She dug around in her backpack. "What about this?" She pulled out the 3rd-eye phone.

The Professor stared at the contraption. "What is it?" he said.

"A phone. I'm going to call Aunt Calista." Uma dialled the number. The phone rang. And rang. And rang. Aunt Calista always turned it off when she was teaching. Uma hung up and closed her eyes. Now what?

"How about sending a text?" the Professor said.

Uma examined the phone. There was no screen and no function button. Apart from supposedly being able to commune with a higher power, the 3rd-eye phone only made calls. "I'll try again."

Again, the phone just rang and rang.

"Is there someone else you could try?" the Professor said.

"Edgar!" Uma stared at the phone. But what was the number for Steve's shop? She had no idea. And she couldn't even call directory enquiries because she didn't know the shop's name. Uma covered her face with her hands. It was something, something Convenience Store.

"Use your mind's eye," Imp said, peering at the top of

Uma's head.

She gave him a glare. Fat help he was. And then he complained when she didn't listen!

"You don't have the number?" Professor Harris said.

"No." Uma had never called Steve before.

Imp appeared on her arm, still clutching a piece of fruit. "*020 7964 2888*," he said with a grin.

"020 7964 2888. How … ?" Uma quickly stopped talking. She'd forgotten Professor Harris was watching.

"The number popped into your head, right?" the Professor said. "Your mom had a strange way of remembering too. She'd call it 'seeing with her mind's eye'. I was never sure whether it was one of her energy talents or some kind of photographic memory."

"Astounding intelligence, in my case." Imp crawled back into Uma's pocket to finish his snack.

Uma dialled the number. After four rings a voice answered. "Steve? It's Uma."

"Hi, it's Edgar."

The truck slowed to a complete stop and strange grinding noises came from all sides.

"Edgar, we've been kidnapped!" Uma said. "We're trapped in a crate and on our way to Peru. You've got to get help!"

"What? Where are you?" Edgar said. "I mean, which airport."

Uma rocked to one side as the crate moved up and across. She landed on the ground with a thud.

"We're being moved into the hold," Imp said. "Can

you smell the aeroplane fuel?"

"I don't know which airport," Uma said. "But we've just arrived."

"It's probably Heathrow," Professor Harris said. "Hurry!"

"Probably Heathrow," Uma told Edgar. "I can't get hold of Aunt Calista. She's teaching at the *Inlighten Centre*, Wimbledon Village. Tell Steve and –"

The line went dead.

"They're here!" Imp burrowed deep into Uma's jacket pocket. "Hide the phone!"

She stuffed the 3rd-eye phone into her bag.

The door creaked open. Two shadows, one thin and wiry the other wide as an ox, stood out against the light.

"Bring in the food and water," Stick said.

Barrel came in carrying a small cardboard box. Stick walked straight across to Uma. She clutched her bag to her chest and he snatched it out of her hands. "What you got in here?" Stick dug around then pulled out the 3rd-eye phone. "What's this?"

Uma watched the lump in the middle of Stick's throat glide up and down his neck. He really didn't seem like the kind of person to lie to. "It's a mobile phone," she said.

Stick threw it back into her bag and dropped the bag onto the floor. "Do you think I'm stupid?" He pushed his face right up against Uma's. She shook her head, too scared to speak.

"Right. So don't try and tell me that thing is a phone."

Stick walked over to Barrel, still pinning her with his angry gaze. "Lying is the kind of mistake you only get to make once."

They turned to leave.

"You can't do this," Uma shouted. "I'll scream and someone will hear!"

"Yeah, you do that." Stick gave a cold laugh before bolting the door on his way out.

Uma opened her mouth and let rip a loud, high scream.

Like an echo, Ginger's piercing screech filled the air. It bounced off the walls and drowned out Uma's cry. Stick had been right to laugh. Screaming wouldn't help.

22

ROAD TRIP

As far as Uma could work out, when it came to utterly useless talents, energy bending was up there with ear wiggling and tune farting. After all, *what* was the upside of being able to walk through walls while cruising at 30,000 feet? None. Not unless she learned how to fly. And Imp had made it pretty clear that flying wasn't on the energy-bending curriculum.

Imp and Professor Harris ate crackers washed down with lemonade but Uma wasn't hungry or thirsty. When Imp dropped asleep head first into a pile of crumbs, she thought he was just being silly. Professor Harris fell asleep soon after. And that was when Uma understood why Aunt Calista had been so worried. Lying rigid on the floor, the Professor muttered and yelled about El Jefe, Izcal, Lake Iticanga and something called the

Vortex. It all sounded as appealing as an Arctic hike in flip-flops.

Uma's eyelids drooped shut, heavy and slow. She lay down on the lumpy, bark-covered floor using her bag as a pillow. The crate was warm, the air lifeless and stale. She felt herself being dragged into a strange, thick sleep, and just as she was slipping under, the Professor shouted out a name: Bartholomew! The word swam in Uma's mind. Who was Bartholomew? And *where* was he?

Hours later, her head still rubbery with sleep, Uma woke as the plane began its juddering descent to land.

It was strange. Even from inside the crate, Uma could tell they were miles and miles from home. "What if Aunt Calista can't get over her flying phobia?" she said to no one in particular.

Imp lay curled in her lap, still half asleep. "I miss Blankie." His voice was soft and dozy. He sat up rubbing his eyes. "Aunt Calista has to fly or abandon you to an unknown fate," he said. "Tough choice."

Uma struggled to properly wake up. "Imp," she said, "we're in serious trouble here. Do you think we could try and work together? You know, like teamwork?"

"Teamwork? Yes!" Imp squinted at Uma. "So you're going to listen to me from now on?"

"Maybe we could listen to each other." Uma turned to Professor Harris whose eyes were open but glazed. He mouthed words noiselessly, still lost in his dreams. "What do you think, Imp? Is he asleep, or awake?"

"Sleep talking," Imp said, using his fingers to comb out his hair. "We should get him up. Barrel and Stick will be here soon." He went over and gently blew into the Professor's face.

Professor Harris lifted his head. "We're landing?"

"Yes." Uma leaned forward and helped him into a sitting position. "Do you know where we are?"

The Professor grinned. "You bet!" He sat up and stretched out his back. "On our way to visit Inca ruins. Though I got to say, flying first class sure isn't what it used to be. Do you think our tour guide is waiting?"

Uma turned to Imp wide-eyed and he lifted a finger, drawing big loops at the side of his head.

The plane wheels pounded onto firm ground and the engine made a keening sound.

The Professor chortled. "Don't worry. I'm just getting into character. You know, senile old man, and all that."

Uma had forgotten. "That's your plan?" Right before falling asleep the Professor had mentioned an idea, a way to avoid being sent into Izcal.

"Sure. A crazy old guy is no use to El Jefe, right?" He looked at Uma, a little embarrassed. "It's not like I'm in any shape to run away or take on Barrel and Stick ... Do you have a better idea?"

"Not yet," Uma said. "I was hoping something would come up, you know, once we're out of this crate."

"Right." The Professor stretched out his legs. "Well, in the meantime," he said, "I'll act doolally. Isn't that what you English call it?"

Clutching the last biscuit from the pack left by Barrel and Stick, Imp jumped into Uma's jacket pocket. "Team work! Let's go!"

Uma took the 3rd-eye phone out of her bag. Apart from a little green light, it didn't work at all. "Guess we just have to stay put until they come for us."

After a while the crate started to move. It shuddered on its way out of the plane.

"OK," the Professor said at the sound of voices. "Lights, camera, action!"

The door swung open. A stream of bright light and the smell of fish, salt and exhaust fumes filled the crate.

"Beautiful sunshine! This is the best time of year to visit," the Professor said cheerfully. "Ah, look! We have a guide AND chauffeur! Well, they did say no expense spared!"

Uma slowly got up. What now? Would they go on another plane, or in a car? How long would it take to reach Izcal? And what would happen when they arrived?

Barrel stood at the crate entrance. "Say bye bye to your travelling companion, we're outta here."

"He means Ginger." Imp looked up at the motionless figure in the tree. "Bye, Ginger! Thanks for sharing!"

Uma took Professor Harris by the hand and steered him to the door. On her way, she picked up the half full bottle of lemonade. Barrel grabbed it out of her hand and threw it into a corner.

"You won't need that no more," he said. "We got what we need in the car."

Outside, Stick was talking to a man dressed in orange overalls. He exchanged a large wad of money for a car key. Stuffing the cash into his pocket, the man left without looking back.

Uma opened her mouth to shout out. Barrel's fat, heavy hand whipped across her face and muffled her scream to a faint whimper. She struggled, trying to bite down on Barrel's podgy fingers, like she'd seen people do in movies, but her jaw was trapped in his grip.

"Don't try any funny business," Barrel growled into her ear before peeling his hand off her face. "Otherwise you'll get some more of that lemonade."

Uma felt sick. The lemonade had been spiked with drugs! That was why they'd slept the whole way over! And if they tried to escape Barrel and Stick would drug them again. Maybe Professor Harris' plan *was* the only hope.

Imp poked Uma's side. "Keep calm," he said. "Get to know the enemy and don't forget you have energy bending."

Uma had to chew the inside of her mouth to stop herself from answering. Imp was being supportive but, really, walking through walls and levitation were turning out to be no use at all.

"Let's go!" Stick waved an arm towards a big jeep.

Smiling, the Professor stepped out of the crate and headed to the car. "This is great! No queues, no baggage reclaim or passport control. These guys sure understand customer service!"

Uma peered out of the hangar and onto the wide airfield. In the distance, through glimmering sunlight, she saw a British Airways plane spilling tourists onto the tarmac.

Barrel's hand thumped down on her shoulder. "Don't even think about it." He opened the jeep door and shoved Uma into the back seat where Professor Harris was gaily clipping shut his seat belt.

As soon as Barrel and Stick got into the front, the doors locked with a clunk.

"I could really do with the bathroom," Professor Harris said.

Stick glared at him in the rear-view mirror. "Sure. Once we're on the road there'll be plenty of bushes to go behind, but until then we're all stuck in this car." He didn't sound too happy. Revving up the engine Stick drove up to a gate held open by the man in orange overalls.

"Where are we going?" Uma said, even though she knew.

Stick looked over his shoulder. "Quiet," he said.

"A real charmer, isn't he?" Imp settled into Uma's lap. "His mother must be so proud."

Uma wasn't ready to be quiet. "Why am I here anyway?"

This time Barrel turned to face the back seat. "El Jefe's orders. But if you don't like it, we can make other arrangements." He made a fist and his knuckles cracked. "If you get my drift."

Uma did. She sat back and closed her eyes. There was no hope of escape until Izcal. And at that point, well, they'd be in the middle of the rainforest. So knowing her enemy wasn't going to help at all.

Night fell as they headed out of the city and down a long coastal road. Stick veered off onto a dirt road for a toilet stop and then kept driving.

Uma was just starting to doze off when Barrel pulled open a cool box and handed out sandwiches and water from the front passenger seat like some domesticated mother gorilla.

Imp sprang into action and raided some M&Ms, stashing them under the seat by Uma's feet. This, Uma supposed, was his idea of teamwork.

Wiping the back of his hand to clean off breadcrumbs, Stick turned to Barrel. "Gimme some of them chocolates."

Barrel dug around in the cool box and pulled out the nearly empty packet. "Hey! You already ate most of 'em!"

"Yeah, blame me, why don't you?" Stick grabbed the pack and dropped it into his lap. "Like we don't already know which one of us has *obesity* issues!"

"You callin' me FAT!" Barrel turned to face Stick. "Just 'cos you're built like a beanpole!"

"Lean and mean." Stick popped a chocolate into his mouth. "And don't think I forgot what happened that time at the all-you-can-eat."

Imp tugged the bottom of Uma's trousers and gave

her a wink. He scrambled up Barrel's seat and dropped a few M&Ms in his lap. It wasn't long before Stick noticed.

"See what I mean!" Stick pointed. "You got some right there!"

"What?" Barrel looked down. "They must've fallen outta the packet. I DID NOT put them there."

"Yeah." Stick stared into the road ahead. "Right."

Barrel turned his back on Stick. "Well, I don't appreciate your *tone*."

The rest of the night was spent in bitter silence.

By daybreak the scenery had changed to dry flatlands and they sped past lagoons festooned with pink flamingos. Professor Harris intermittently burst into commentaries about Peruvian customs, folklore and sights. Stick just kept driving.

During the afternoon they travelled through the Urubamba valley past a massive camping ground full of tents.

"Are we staying here?" Uma said.

Stick flashed a stare into the rear-view mirror. "What da you think?"

As night fell, the road got bumpier until the jeep finally came to a stop.

Barrel and Stick climbed out of the car and began unloading the boot. Uma stared through the window at the big square of ground stripped back to make a campsite where two shed-sized tents had already been set up. A forest of towering green trees surrounded the clearing. Other than the track the only way in or out was through the jungle.

"Ah," Professor Harris said, opening the car door, "the Peruvian rainforest." An ecstatic smile spread across his face as he pointed through the half-light to a low, rectangular building that bordered the camp. It was made of ancient stone blocks. "And some kind of temple," he said. "I wonder if our guides know something about its history."

Stick dropped a heavy box outside one of the tents. "Are you for real?" He shook his head. "This is Izcal."

Professor Harris smiled. "Izcal? How interesting! I've never heard of the place."

23

IZCAL

"Wha' da ya mean, never heard of the place?" Barrel snarled like a chained Rottweiler.

Professor Harris smiled sweetly, apparently lost in his own world. "I've visited quite a few Inca ruins, but none in this area. It's a much smaller temple than any of the others I've seen."

Stick loudly unzipped a tent. "He probably don't recognise the place since El Jefe had the track and camp cleared!"

Barrel eyed the Professor suspiciously. "Do you think we got the wrong guy?"

Professor Harris wandered into the undergrowth and began collecting branches. "I'll get the fire going!"

Barrel and Stick exchanged a look.

Imp chuckled. He hadn't left Uma's pocket since they'd all got out of the car. "It's taken those goons this long to notice Professor Harris might not be all there."

Uma sat on her backpack at the base of the temple. Trees and plant-life erupted from where the clearing ended – dense, green and murky. The drive from the main road had taken maybe thirty minutes. And it had been over a rough track, so they hadn't been going fast. If she managed to get away unnoticed – and that was a big IF – how long would it take to walk back?

Stick dropped a box on the ground. "Forget the camp fire," he said when Professor Harris started rubbing two sticks together. "It ain't even cold."

"But it'll help keep away wild animals, jaguars for example." The Professor looked up from his work. "And Inca spirits."

Barrel set down a big cardboard box. "What do ya mean?"

The Professor looked up as though surely everyone knew about Inca spirits. "This thing here," the Professor pointed at the temple, "is a funerary monument."

Uma stared at the box-shaped temple made of large slabs of rock. At first, she'd thought it was totally plain but looking more closely she realised that some of the rock was carved. Each of the bottom corners showed the writhing, open-jawed head of a dragon spewing fire. And at the top centre of the front wall there was a sun with swirly, snaking rays, just like the one Professor Harris had drawn on the back of Mum and Dad's picture. Plain or not, there was something special about the temple. It had a sort of glow, and felt like a solid, safe presence. A bit how she imagined standing next to Dad would feel.

"A fune-what kinda monument?" Barrel said.

Stick spat on the ground. "He means dead people."

"Not just ordinary dead people!" the Professor said. "Warrior kings fallen in battle who roam the night to avenge their death by killing any human they find." The Professor looked up with wide eyes. "Didn't you know?"

Barrel stepped forward. "Here, I gotta lighter."

"Yeah well, I don't believe in no fairy tales." Stick dragged a stack of sleeping bags from the car as though he couldn't care less.

Imp scrambled onto Uma's shoulder and tugged her hair. "Notice how he's stopped arguing about the campfire, though?" he said.

"See those carved dragons?" Professor Harris continued. "They represent Chuichu, the rainbow god. The Inca believed that rainbows connected the human world to the godly world. Another time, I'll tell you stories about 'hoocha'. It's what the Inca called *dark energy*." The Professor turned to Uma and gave her a secret wink. "For example, if you look closely," he said to Barrel and Stick, "you'll see the temple has no entrance."

Stick dropped a sleeping bag.

Barrel looked excited. "Yeah! That's why El Jefe had us looking for you! To get us into that place! 'Course he's tried to find other ways in too."

Stick slapped the side of Barrel's head. "Shut up! You don't gotta tell 'em everything!"

"What does it matter if he knows?" Rubbing his ear, Barrel picked the sleeping bag off the floor.

Professor Harris wiped his hands and sat back to enjoy the campfire. "So who is El Jefe? And will he be joining our excursion?"

Barrel and Stick exchanged another look.

"Don't be embarrassed!" The Professor chuckled. "I realised the truth a long time ago!"

Uma sat up to listen. Where was the Professor going with this?

"Oh yeah," Stick said. "What truth is that?"

"You're not tour guides, are you? I mean it's clear you don't know much."

Barrel and Stick didn't answer. It was as though they were trying to figure out whether the Professor was completely insane or having them on.

"You're just the drivers," the Professor explained. "El Jefe's our guide, right?"

Stick laughed. "Yeah, that's right." He threw two sleeping bags into each of the tents. "El Jefe arrives tomorrow and is gonna take you on a nice little trip. But now it's sleepy time, and, see, I'm fresh outta hot cocoa though I'll make sure to get some from the store tomorrow."

"Ouch," Imp muttered into Uma's ear. "That really is an astonishing level of sarcasm."

Stick waved an arm, pointing. "Now, both of ya, get into that tent. I don't wanna hear no more stories about tour guides or deadly spirits."

"Yeah," Barrel said, stoking the fire. "That kinda stuff gives me nightmares."

Professor Harris stood up and headed for the tent. "You should know that the 'hoocha' spirits have a very distinctive cry. A deep roar followed by a high-pitched whistling sound – unmistakable. If you hear that, make sure to stay close to the fire." The Professor stopped before going into the tent. "You will be here to protect us, won't you?"

Stick guffawed. "Oh yeah, right outside, making sure nothing gets in."

"Good." The Professor gave a small bow. "Thank you. We'll get some rest now."

Uma followed Professor Harris into the tent and Stick zipped it closed. "We'll be right out here," he said, "protectin' ya!"

The tent was dark, lit only by the faint light that came from the campfire. Uma felt Imp jump out of her pocket. He had no problem seeing in the dark, and had probably gone to claim his corner of the tent. Or search for snacks.

"Professor Harris," Uma whispered, "we need to get away before El Jefe arrives."

The Professor unravelled his sleeping bag and climbed in. "No. *You* need to get away," he said. "Barrel and Stick seem to be falling for my play-acting, and so long as they have me, they won't bother following you. This may be your only chance to get away before El Jefe arrives."

158

"Right." Uma unzipped her sleeping bag. Did the Professor really expect her to find her way alone?

Professor Harris leaned over. "Just follow the track onto the main road," he said in an urgent whisper, "it shouldn't take much longer than an hour. Then hide until early morning. There's not much traffic, but a tourist bus should go past at some point. Flag one down and stay away from passenger cars. Do you understand?"

Uma nodded. He was serious. A tight knot gnawed at her stomach lining and mushroomed into her chest until she could hardly breathe. Was she really going out there on her own? "What about jaguars and stuff?"

"Your biggest concern is Lancehead snakes hidden in leaves, but the track is pretty clear. Just be careful. Jaguars don't come near humans, so apart from snakes you just have to worry about insects. Keep covered, especially at dawn."

Uma's chest felt tight, as though she'd developed a sudden case of acute pneumonia.

"You're not safe here," the Professor said. If El Jefe finds out about the walking through walls thing, he'll take you *in there*." The Professor pointed at the temple as though it led to the gates of hell.

"Take *me* in? I don't understand what you – " Uma broke off as she realised.

On the plane, right before she'd got distracted by the idea of walking out of the crate, Professor Harris had said he didn't have the key to Izcal *'until now'*.

"I'm the key," she whispered. Izcal was a walled tomb

with no entrance. Only Uma could get El Jefe in. Like Mum must have got Dad and the Professor through.

Professor Harris looked puzzled. "Yes. I already explained. Didn't you – "

"What about when El Jefe finds out you can't get him into Izcal? That you're no use to him."

"Enough with the whispers!" Stick barked from just outside the tent flap.

Professor Harris grabbed Uma's hot hands. "Get as far away from here as you can. And get help," he said. "I have total faith you can do this."

"OK." Uma wished she shared the Professor's total faith. She snuggled deep into the sleeping bag and covered her head, green with fear at going into the night alone. And what would happen to Professor Harris when she'd gone?

Imp pushed up against her face and she stroked his head, speaking in a whisper. "What do *you* think we should do?"

"Uma Marilyn Collins," Imp said, "are you actually asking my advice?"

"Yeah well, just this once."

Imp took a deep breath and sighed. "The Professor's right, we have to leave as soon as those two thugs are asleep."

Uma had hoped Imp would come up with something more cunning. "Isn't there an energy-bending thing I can do?"

"Maybe one day years from now you'll be able to

transmogrifly, but right now," Imp shrugged, "no hope."

"Transmogrifly?"

"Forget it," Imp said. "Transmogriflycation is when you transport yourself from one place to another by dissolving and reintegrating your material field in time and space."

Uma hadn't understood a word. "*What?*"

"Yes, exactly." Imp sounded worried. "Look, I'll be happy if you can get us out through the back of the tent."

"I can do that," Uma said, even though she hadn't managed to walk through anything since Fir Lodge.

"Good. Make sure you stay awake." Imp curled into the crook of her neck. "I'm going to catch a few Z's."

Uma didn't argue because sleep would be impossible. She chewed a strand of hair and tried to slow her breathing. Wimbledon was a long way away, and so was Aunt Calista.

How would she ever get home safe?

24

INTO THE MOONLIGHT

Uma listened as the rummaging and talking gradually died down. Moonlight bathed the tent in an eerie glow and she could make out Barrel's grizzly-bear shadow settling into position outside.

The temple's stark outline formed a silhouette against the tent walls. Even though El Jefe would soon arrive expecting to take Professor Harris into Izcal, Uma wasn't scared. Not even the screeching of night birds was frightening. It was weird, but she felt safe in this strange, unfamiliar place. It was as though the moonlight reflecting off the temple walls was somehow creating a secure, luminous bubble. Uma wiped her face. Her hands were burning even though the night air was cold.

Imp tugged her hair. "I think we can go."

"You mean they're properly asleep?" Uma said, in

her tiniest whisper.

A deep, rumbling snore rose from Barrel's chest and echoed into the jungle. The rumble was followed by a high-pitched whistle coming from Stick's tent.

"Er, yeah – I would say so." Imp pushed open the sleeping bag zipper. "Though it sounds just like the hoocha Professor Harris talked about."

Uma wriggled free, trying not to make noise. She grabbed her bag and pulled it over her shoulders. The 3rd-eye phone hadn't been much use so far but might still come in handy. Like if she needed something heavy to throw.

Imp climbed onto Uma's shoulder. "Can you manage?"

She nodded and leaned over Professor Harris. He was breathing deeply, eyes shut and jaw slack. Was it right to leave him? What if she couldn't get help in time?

The Professor's eyes sprang wide open and Uma had to hold back a scream. He grabbed her hand. "Don't go," he whispered, pulling Uma close.

His fingers tightened around her wrist and Uma recoiled. Was he properly awake? Or having a nightmare?

He dragged her closer until they were face to face. "Don't go near the Vortex. It will kill you," he said. The whites of his eyes glowed in the moonlight and she felt his breath on her cheek.

"I won't," she said. "We're going – I mean, *I'm* going to get help, remember?" She prised open his fingers and laid the Professor's hand gently on his chest. He turned away and closed his eyes. Uma didn't think he'd heard.

"Freaky," Imp said, shuddering. "He was having another nightmare."

Uma tiptoed to the back of the tent, lifted a hand and laid it on the cold fabric wall. Her fingers tingled and the centre of her palms burned. Uma didn't know why but for the first time ever, she felt sure about doing energy bending. "Let's go."

Without hesitating or even a moment's thought, Uma stepped forward. When she set her foot down it hit the damp rainforest floor and she felt the scurry of a small animal head for cover.

"Brilliant! " Imp said. "You're getting the hang of this!"

Uma grinned. It had felt natural, as though her whole body had turned to air and re-formed on the other side of the tent wall. And this time it was no fluke – she'd actually made it happen! Uma wiped her clammy hands over her jacket.

Imp glanced nervously towards Barrel's sleeping figure. "Shame you haven't mastered disappearing. It would be pretty useful, right about now."

Uma clutched the strap of her backpack and slowly edged past Barrel, the campfire and Stick's tent.

Then she had an idea and stopped. She turned back and crept towards the dying embers of the campfire.

Imp tugged her hair frantically. "What are you doing?"

Uma didn't answer. She was too scared to even

whisper. The soft, moist ground cushioned her footsteps as she slinked towards Stick's backpack. She'd seen him put the car key in the front pouch. Her fingers rummaged and coins jingled.

"Shhhh," Imp hissed. "*Please* shhhh!"

Uma gently used the tips of her fingers to find the key's shape and weight. But as she eased it out of the pouch, the button squeezed down and a shrill BEEP-BEEP tore through the silence shrouding the camp. Uma stood rigid, holding her breath.

There was a stutter in the whistling that came from Stick's tent.

Barrel lumbered to one side, snorted and sat up.

In a reflex that came from nowhere, Uma held her hands over her eyes. As though that would mean Barrel wouldn't see her standing right in the middle of camp! She waited, expecting a shout, or the sound of Barrel lumbering to his feet. But all she heard was the distant flutter of a bird's wings.

Uma was scared to look. She slowly opened a slit between her fingers and saw Barrel staring right at her – but somehow through her, as though she were camouflaged by the night. Glowing in the silvery light, Barrel's round face looked like a second, smaller moon – one with a puzzled expression.

Uma slowed her breath so that even her chest barely moved.

Barrel wiped a hand over his face, crashed onto the sleeping bag and turned his back on Uma, curling into a tight ball.

"Awesome," Imp said, "you've done the disappearing thing!"

For a moment, Uma didn't understand what he meant. Then she dropped her hands and held them out in front of her face. They were gone! She looked down at her feet. Completely not there! Imp was right – she'd disappeared herself. But how? By hiding her eyes? Although Uma couldn't see her hands, she could feel them burning red hot. It was because of being near Izcal. Uma was sure of it.

"Why the car key?" Imp said. "Can you drive?"

Uma pulled a face. What 11-year old could drive? No – confiscating the car key might buy some time if Barrel and Stick noticed she'd gone. Uma hurried past the temple and away from camp. She wasn't sure how far sound carried in the jungle so walked in silence, down the middle of the dirt track, watching out for piles of leaves.

As they got further away, instead of feeling safe, Uma felt more scared. Everything was darker, colder and more sinister this far from the temple.

"I'm worried about Professor Harris," Uma said after about twenty minutes. "What if we can't get help?"

"We'll get help. We have to." Imp lay across Uma's shoulder, his head resting in the crook of her neck. "You know, I had no idea the rainforest would be this LOUD at night. All I can hear is the chirping, buzzing and snuffling of animals."

Uma hurried alongside the shadowy trees. She wished that instead of the car key, she'd had the sense to take some water or food. It wouldn't be long before Imp started going on about the effects of dehydration and food deprivation.

Uma sighed. "Did you feel a glow around the temple?"

There was no answer. Instead, he gave Uma's hair a tug. "I think we should get away from the track. El Jefe will be coming this way."

Uma freed her hair from his grip. "No way I'm heading into the rainforest. We'll get lost. And anyway, it's not far to the main road."

"Maybe," Imp said, pulling her ear lobe, "but we should stay hidden."

Uma swatted Imp's hand away from her ear. "Why? Even if El Jefe does come, we'll hear his car well before he has a chance to see me." Uma peered through the silvery light into the rainforest. The trees were packed closely together and she was sure that snakes were slithering in the undergrowth.

Imp gave Uma a sharp pinch on the back of her neck. "Why don't you ever listen to me? *You* said 'teamwork'!"

Uma gritted her teeth and kept walking along the track. "Stop being a bully! You can't poke and pinch me like I'm made of straw."

"I'm *trying* to help." Imp climbed off her shoulder onto a low-hanging branch. He glared at Uma. "But you never learn."

"WHAT? *I* don't learn? Are you *serious*?" Uma said.

"Now get off there, we need to go."

Imp put his hands on his hips. "We should get well away from the track."

Uma shook her head in disbelief. "No. We need to get help as soon as possible, without getting lost."

"No." Imp sat on the branch, crossed his legs and rested his chin in his hand.

Uma hid her face in her hands. Could this be happening? Was Imp really creating a problem NOW, in the middle of the night, and HERE, in the middle of the rainforest? "What do you mean, 'no'?" she said. "Let's go, now!"

Imp stared Uma down. "I am right about this. And I won't get off the branch until you agree."

Uma felt a surge of blood pump up her neck and into her cheeks. Her eyes watered with fury. "Yes, and that's exactly what this is about. You being *right!*" She stared at Imp's truculent, uncooperative face. "Actually, the problem is that *everything* is always about *you!* I mean, why can't you butt out long enough for me to finish a normal conversation? Why couldn't you just have been nice to Edgar? And why do you always think *your* way is best? Or the *only* way?"

"I help too, you know!" Imp said. "But nothing I do seems to *count!*"

Uma kicked the ground at her feet. "That's it, I'm done! From now on you stay home, even if I have to lock you in a box!" She turned her back on Imp. "And now we're going to the main road." Furious, she walked away without waiting for Imp to catch up.

25

TRACKED

Uma strode down the track. She'd already been walking nearly an hour – the main road couldn't be far. Imp was sulking, of course. He hadn't spoken at all since their argument, but that was his usual way.

After a couple more minutes Uma heard the distinct hum of a car. She stopped still, listening. It was getting closer. Definitely.

"El Jefe," Uma whispered. She scurried off the path and into the undergrowth. Now they really were out of time. It wouldn't be long before El Jefe reached camp – and found out that Professor Harris couldn't get him into Izcal.

From behind the narrow trunk of a rubber tree, Uma saw a pair of dimmed headlights. She hid, waiting for the car to drive past. But it didn't. The car stopped. Uma scurried a few steps deeper into the rainforest, watching to see what would happen next.

She heard the sound of a car door open, and a man's voice drifted through the night. "Uma! I know you're out here."

Everything was outlined in the moonlight: the car, the silhouette of every tree, and El Jefe holding an oval-shaped box at his side. *How* could he know where she was? It didn't make sense. Even if Barrel and Stick had told him that she'd got away, *how* could he know to stop exactly *here*?

El Jefe held out an arm and a sudden, bright light swept up, probing the trees. Uma quickly lifted her hands over her eyes. She needed to disappear, but her palms didn't feel hot any more, not even warm.

The air around Uma's face brightened as the torch's glow landed on her head.

"Don't move!" El Jefe shouted. "You're coming with me." He sounded pleased, almost a little surprised, as though he'd won against the odds.

Uma looked down at her feet. The disappearing hadn't worked! She edged slowly backwards, deeper into the jungle.

"There's no point running," El Jefe said. His voice was calm and cold.

Uma stumbled over a tree root and fled.

El Jefe crashed into the undergrowth. "Don't run!" His command was sharp and threatening, like the bark of a Rottweiler. "I'll only find you."

The tree cover got thicker as Uma headed deeper

into the jungle. Just like Imp had wanted her to do in the first place.

"Stop!"

Uma heard El Jefe's bark ring through the trees, muffled by the sound of her panting breath. Legs burning, she kept running. Worried about getting lost, Uma looked up at the sky and searched for a guiding star. But everything shook and moved as she pelted forward. After a few minutes, she doubled over, a stitch tearing at the side of her waist.

She couldn't hear El Jefe at all.

Uma looked around. She needed a place to hide. And there, only a few steps away, was a wide, hollow trunk with a gap large enough to crawl into. But what if some other creature was already hiding in the space? Uma edged closer, picked a stick off the ground and used it to poke around inside the hole. Nothing stirred. She slowly edged half way in and waited. Everything was quiet. Uma squeezed all the way into the hollow trunk, curled her knees tight into her chest and buried her head in her arms. Right now there was no animal scarier than El Jefe. He wouldn't find her hiding place, but how long before he gave up looking? Even though it was probably too late, Uma had to at least try and get help for Professor Harris. But how long before it was safe to leave?

Uma's head sprang up. A sound. From close by. She held her breath and waited. Was it El Jefe?

Something whipped into the hollow and yanked

Uma's hair. She fell forward with a scream.

Uma tried to scramble upright. Clumps of hair tore out of her scalp as she was dragged out of her hiding place. "I told you not to run," El Jefe snarled.

Uma didn't understand. How could he have found her so easily?

El Jefe shone his torch into her face and the light made her eyes water. With one final yank, he pulled Uma to her feet. Triumphant, El Jefe held the oval box she'd seen earlier right up in front of her face. "Say 'thank you, Aunt Calista,'" El Jefe said with a smirk. "It's incredible that this thing works."

What did he mean?

El Jefe snorted with contempt. "Your aunt was using this," he held up the oval box, "to track your phone. It's quite the homing device." He grabbed Uma's arm and dragged her on. "At least, that's what they were doing until I put a stop to them."

"Them?" Uma said.

"Yeah, your aunt, her boyfriend and that kid. But they won't be causing me any more trouble."

Uma blinked hard to stop tears from filling her eyes. "Where are they?"

El Jefe moved his grip off Uma's arm and held her round the neck. She could already feel the bruise his fingers were making. "They're alive," he said, "if that's what you're worried about. Now it's up to you whether or not they stay that way."

"What have you done to them?" she said, in a hoarse

whisper.

Still holding her neck, El Jefe dug a hand into Uma's back and pushed her along. "Let's just say they've a had some 'lemonade' to make them more cooperative."

Uma tried to pull away. They'd almost reached the track and she could see the car – its door still open. If she could escape El Jefe's grip she could lock herself in the car. Maybe even drive away. Could driving be that difficult? They got closer and Uma kicked El Jefe hard in the shin. Instead of letting go, his fingers dug deeper into her neck. A tearing pain around Uma's windpipe made it impossible to breath. She struggled, gagged and choked.

El Jefe pressed her head down and pushed her hard into the back of the car. Uma crashed into the side of the door opposite and landed face down, disoriented. She heard El Jefe open the glove compartment. He reached back and grabbed her arm. A tiny stab pierced her skin and liquid sleep spread through her veins and into her brain.

It was over. She was powerless. If she'd listened to Imp then maybe … Imp? Through the fog that drifted into her head, Uma realised something awful. She used her last strength to push her hands deep into her pockets and dig around.

Imp wasn't sulking. He was gone.

26

WHO'S IN, WHO'S OUT?

Uma didn't know how long she'd been asleep. She felt as though her brain had been coated in treacle, and her eyes stuck with super-glue. Slowly, memories blended together to form a picture. She was in Peru with Professor Harris. She'd been drugged again and … she felt sick with panic. Aunt Calista? What had happened to Aunt Calista and the others? Uma felt into her pockets. And Imp. Where was Imp?

Uma sat onto her elbows and prised open her eyes. The grey tent wall. And sounds of talking. She tried to stand. Impossible. Her hands and feet were strapped with white plastic strips. She focused on the voices. It sounded like Barrel in rumbling conversation with Professor Harris. Every now and then El Jefe barked out an order. Then she heard the sound of a woman's voice.

Aunt Calista! It had to be!

"I'm here!" Uma shouted. "Help me! I'm here!"

Footsteps approached and the tent flap was pulled wide open. El Jefe stood in the entrance. "Help?" he said. "No one can help you now." He reached out and grabbed Uma by an arm, pulling her up. She wavered, struggling to balance on feet that couldn't sit flat on the ground. Out of the corner of one eye, Uma saw the flash of a blade. El Jefe lunged toward her and she flinched.

Relief. Her ankles straightened and Uma stood upright. El Jefe had cut the tie. He dragged her out of the tent. Aunt Calista, then Steve, Professor Harris and Edgar sat, trussed and lined up against the temple wall.

"Uma!" Aunt Calista's face was streaked with dirt and tears. "I'm so sorry," she said, trying to sit up. "The 3rd-eye phone ... it's my fault you were caught!"

Uma stumbled forward, pushed along by El Jefe. She gave Aunt Calista a small smile. "But you found me," she said. "And I'm so glad you're here."

El Jefe pushed Uma onto the ground, next to Edgar.

"OK," El Jefe said. "This is how it's going to play out. You," he pointed at Uma, "are coming with me, and YOU, will stay here until I'm back." He waved the gun at the others.

Aunt Calista struggled to stand. "You can't take Uma! And what do you mean 'back'? Where are you going?"

El Jefe pointed at the temple. "We're going to Iticanga, the place Mommy and Daddy were looking for. And *she's* going to get me there."

Uma leaned forward and stared at Professor Harris dumbfounded. How did El Jefe know she was the key? Had Professor Harris been forced to tell?

Edgar shouted. "You can't! It's dangerous in there!"

Steve reached out, trying to grab Aunt Calista's hands. "I'll go," he said. "Take me instead."

El Jefe smirked. "None of you are any use to me."

"Uma can't help!" Aunt Calista said. "She doesn't know anything about her Mum and Dad's research. I'll take you!"

"You?" El Jefe looked at Aunt Calista doubtfully. "Can you get me in there?"

"Yes! Let's go." Aunt Calista scuffled forward on her bottom. "Untie me!"

El Jefe smirked. "You know, until Uma got Professor Harris out of Fir Lodge, it didn't cross my mind it was a family thing."

Aunt Calista looked confused. "What do you mean?"

"You knew we were there?" Uma said. "How? You didn't see us."

"I know all about Mommy's powers and the Professor couldn't have got out of that room without help – and then he disappeared. That's when I really started watching Uma." El Jefe waved the gun. "She's quite the budding talent."

"I don't understand." Aunt Calista spoke in a whisper. "What happened at Fir Lodge?"

Uma swallowed hard. "Nothing."

"Uma Marilyn Collins," Aunt Calista said. "Can you

walk through walls?"

Edgar rested his head on bent knees. "What's going on?"

"He's making things up," Uma said. "Walking through walls? That's mad." Total denial seemed like the best option.

Aunt Calista stared at the floor for a second, then looked across at Uma. "It's not mad because that's the kind of thing your Mum could do."

"What?" Steve said.

Edgar lifted his head. "What?"

"WHAT?" Uma echoed. There really was nothing else to say. "You know about Mum?"

"Of course – I was there when it happened!" Aunt Calista pulled a hand through her hair. "But *you* know?" she said, "How? Since when?"

"Not long," Uma said through a half-locked jaw. "Why didn't you tell me?"

Aunt Calista hung her head. "After our Dad died, your Mum couldn't do anything energy-wise for months and months. She always said you had incredible abilities but I never saw any so assumed you lost them when *your* parents died. What was the point telling you something so incredible when you didn't remember anything yourself?"

"I can't believe it." Uma's voice squeaked like a mouse on helium. If she'd listened to Imp about energy bending then Aunt Calista might have told her about Mum. Ages ago.

El Jefe clicked his fingers in front of Aunt Calista's face. "This is all very nice," he said, "but we need to go."

Aunt Calista didn't move.

Her face turned powder white.

El Jefe grabbed her by the arm and dragged her up. "Now!" His voice was cold as death.

Aunt Calista slumped back against the temple wall. "Sorry, Uma ... I didn't get ..." Aunt Calista paused, "I don't have ... what I mean is, I can't actually walk through walls. Sorry Uma, I can't help."

Edgar snorted. Steve made a weird, strangled sound, that might have been 'don't worry, neither can I'.

El Jefe grabbed her face in one hand. "But you were there!"

"Yes, but I was downstairs," Aunt Calista hung her head. "All I got was this crazy-coloured hair!"

So the fluorescent pink was an accident but not the kind involving hair colour. It made sense. Such a violent shade of fuchsia could never have come out of a box.

El Jefe stared at Aunt Calista. "OK, so I'll take the girl." He waved his gun.

"No!" Edgar threw himself across Uma and she felt his hand slip into her pocket – then Edgar slumped back. El Jefe had whacked him on the head and a bloody welt was already swelling at his hairline. Uma curled her fingers around the cold weight of Edgar's Swiss Army knife.

Aunt Calista pulled him onto her lap and examined the wound. "How could you hit a child?" she said.

El Jefe snorted as though Aunt Calista had said something funny. Then he pulled Uma back onto her feet. "You know, all those years I thought Harris had some kind of key or code to get into the temple. Now I know it's actually this kid! I could've brought her here way back." He cut the tie around Uma's wrists then turned to Barrel and Stick. "Harvey! Lionel! I'm taking the girl, you stay with these people." He glowered at his henchmen through drooped lids. "And no sleeping on the job."

Barrel and Stick hurried closer, scared and eager to redeem themselves.

El Jefe dragged Uma away. "Say goodbye."

"No!" Aunt Calista yelled. "You can't do this!"

Uma stumbled. "It's alright. I'll be fine!" she yelled. This was her fault. They were all here because she'd rushed into Fir Lodge without a plan. And because she'd never believed Imp about energy bending ... Uma chewed the inside of her mouth. And now Imp was gone, maybe eaten by an anaconda or mauled by a jungle rat, just because she hadn't listened.

Professor Harris, face grey, eyes wide, struggled to stand. "I'll come too," he said. "I know the dangers! Let me come!"

Uma grabbed El Jefe by the arm. "No," she said. "He'll slow us down. Let's just go." Izcal would kill Professor Harris – and none of this was his fault.

"Yeah, good choice." El Jefe pushed Uma towards the tents and picked up a backpack. "Is everything in here?"

he said to Barrel.

"Yes, sir. I packed it all like you said."

El Jefe took a thick coil of rope from the floor, tightened it first round Uma's waist and then his own. "Let's go."

Uma followed El Jefe to the side of the temple. Professor Harris was trying to stand by pushing his back against the wall and slowly pulling himself upright. Aunt Calista nursed Edgar while Steve looked helplessly on.

"Come on," El Jefe said. "Do your thing."

Uma put one hand on the temple wall. There was something special about the place, maybe because Mum and Dad had been here. And whatever happened next she was following in their footsteps.

Something brushed against the side of Uma's ankle. She looked down and saw a strange, furry creature. It had the face and tail of a squirrel but the body of a rabbit. The animal's head twitched as Imp sat upright on its back. He was riding the squirrel-rabbit as though it were some kind of fluffy horse! Imp grinned and gave Uma a salute.

"What are you waiting for?" El Jefe growled. He followed Uma's gaze to the ground. "Oh. That thing." He lifted his foot and gave the animal a kick.

The creature ran away and Imp tumbled to the ground. He sprang to his feet and scrabbled up Uma's clothes to her shoulder. "Did you miss me?" he said.

"I'm really sorry." Uma didn't care if El Jefe thought

she was talking to herself.

"Too late for that," El Jefe said. "Come on. Let's go."

Imp gently pulled Uma's hair. "Teamwork?" he said. "But really, this time?"

"Teamwork!" Uma grinned and pushed a hand into the stone. She couldn't rely on her energy bending powers – but at least Imp was back.

Anyway, Professor Harris had somehow survived Izcal ... maybe she could too.

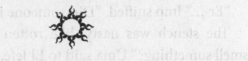

27

AURORA

The dark was thick and icy. Uma felt as though she'd stepped into a metal coffin buried at the bottom of the sea. Crisp air singed the inside of her nose and, deep in the profound silence, she heard her breath crackle as it froze.

Imp wound a thick strand of Uma's hair around his neck and shoulders. He shivered. *"Who turned off the heating?"*

El Jefe stood at Uma's elbow. "There's supposed to be a cavern of lights," he said. Do you see anything?"

Uma couldn't even make out a silhouette. Or the fingers held in front of her face. "This is the opposite of a cavern of lights."

The cord around Uma's waist rubbed when El Jefe pulled the bag off his shoulders. "Professor Harris said there would be a rainbow light," he said in a too-loud voice, as though excitement was bursting out of his mouth. There was a soft, patting sound as El Jefe tapped his jacket pocket. "I took notes. And I've read them so often, I thought I knew what was coming."

"Er …" Imp sniffed. "Did someone just … ?"

The stench was nasty, like rotten eggs. "Can you smell something?" Uma said to El Jefe.

"Of course," he dropped his bag to the floor. "I'm getting my torch."

Uma took a small step back and reached through the dark for the temple wall. There was nothing but cold and empty space.

Curling her fingers around the metal of Edgar's army knife, Uma moved away. All she had to do was find a wall, cut the rope and jump through. El Jefe would be trapped in Izcal and she would be safe.

But the wall wasn't there. Uma took one more step back and El Jefe grabbed her arm.

"What are you doing?" His breath was hot on her cheek

Uma's eyes blinked in the dark. "I can't feel the wall," she said. "What if we're trapped?"

"Don't worry about that now." El Jefe dropped a hand on her shoulder. "Let's just get to Iticanga first."

There was a click as he switched on the torch. Then cracking, banging and fizzing sprang out of the dark. Coloured lights popped, shot, whizzed through the air, high up and right in front of her face: red, orange, blue, magenta. The lights were bright, alive and vibrant. As loud as fireworks crashing inside her head. Imp clung to Uma's neck as she crouched down, and El Jefe held the torch in front of his body like a dagger.

"Yeah," he said, "that's more like it." El Jefe slowly scanned the area but, other than exploding lights, there was nothing. No wall, no ceiling, no path, just an endless black hole lit by a multi-coloured firestorm.

Imp tugged Uma's hair. "Should I go and scout?"

"No. Let's stick together." With so much noise, Uma didn't think El Jefe could hear her talk to Imp. And, anyway, so what if he thought she was mad?

A red flare skimmed past Uma's face and suddenly there was a new smell. From somewhere really close by. She pulled a hand through her hair and the ends snapped away, dry and brittle. Singed flakes fell to the floor. "Imp? Are you alright?" He'd been sitting on her shoulder, but where was he now? Uma checked the floor. She felt a ripple in her pocket.

"Not nice," Imp wailed. "Look!" He pointed at a small, smoking hole in his trousers.

"This stuff is dangerous," Uma said. "What should we do?"

El Jefe yanked her arm, hard. "What are you saying?"

He was right by her side but still Uma had to shout. "The lights burn!" she said. "Are you sure this is right?"

"What?" El Jefe had covered his ears.

"The lights burn!" A streak of yellow flashed past Uma's head and she ducked away. This was like being holed up in the trenches.

El Jefe came closer. "Is there nothing you can do?"

"We need shelter," Imp said.

"We should find shelter," Uma shouted.

"No." Multi-coloured flecks lit El Jefe's pupils. "Harris said the rainbow showed the way." He dragged Uma by the elbow. A green fireball jetted towards their heads; fast and targeted, like a rocket set on Destruct.

Uma veered away, holding her hands up in a useless reflex. As though willpower was enough to ward off a burning missile. Squeezing shut her eyes she waited for the searing light to scorch her skin.

There was a shriek and the rope around Uma's waist yanked hard, pulling her to the ground. She landed with a thud.

"Aaaaahhh!" El Jefe's face glistened with sweat and he clutched a shoulder. The forearm was blistered, and wisps of smoke rose from his charred shirt.

The lights kept on exploding. Uma pulled open El Jefe's backpack, took out a water bottle and emptied it over the wound.

"Aaaaahhh!" El Jefe rolled onto his side and curled into a ball. "Do something," he whispered. "Just do something."

Uma reached into her pocket for Imp. He clung to her finger like a baby and she gently stroked his head. No wonder Professor Harris hadn't wanted to come back to Izcal. "What can I do, Imp?"

Imp stuffed bits of tissue in his ear. "Try deflection," he said.

"What's that?" Uma jumped as a searing purple rocket flashed past her face.

"The opposite of levitation. Instead of drawing something close, repulse it. Just try," he said.

El Jefe groaned as he pulled his arm close into his chest. "Stop yakking to yourself and do something."

A yellow streak landed on the floor, just missing Uma's trouser leg. She held her hands over her head, palms up. Now what? Uma closed her eyes and imagined the crashing lights move away, deflected by an invisible force shooting out of her hands. She yelped as a sharp pain burned into her palms. It hadn't worked. She'd been hit!

Imp poked his head over the top of her pocket. "Pretty good," he said. "Guess that means it's safe to come out."

Uma checked her hands. They weren't burnt but instead, a strange circle of hot, white light throbbed in each palm. The fireworks burst, crashed and thundered same as before – but from a distance. She looked up and saw a film of light that had formed a protective shield above their heads. Uma grinned. She'd done it!

El Jefe pushed the First Aid kit into Uma's hands. "Good job. I wasn't sure you had it in you." He groaned, reached into his jacket and pulled out his gun. "Drugs first," he said, "then dressing."

Uma wished El Jefe's legs had been injured instead of his arm. At least then it would have been worth *trying* to escape. Gun or no gun. She gave him some painkillers and water then ripped open a pack of sterile dressing. She wound it round El Jefe's arm.

He turned his head to one side and closed his eyes. Uma could see tears of pain glisten between his eyelashes. "This has to work," he said.

"I'm doing my best," Uma said, thinking he meant the bandage.

El Jefe winced. "Everything's riding on this project." He turned to Uma and stared at her with cold, dark eyes. "You know, a few days after Harris left my clinic the whole place burned down." He looked at the black blisters on his arm. "My life's work. Gone. I was homeless; penniless until the insurance money came through." He grabbed Uma's arm. "Do you know what that feels like? To have nothing?" His face twisted into a bitter snarl and he looked away. "No. Of course you don't."

Uma tied a knot at the top of the bandage. She didn't think misfortune was an excuse. "Now what?"

El Jefe looked around. "The lights lead the way. Unless you got a better idea? Something your Mom would have done?"

"Let's see." Uma looked at the shield over their heads. "At least now it's safe to explore."

El Jefe tugged the rope around Uma's waist. "There." He pointed at a line of orange sparkles. They seemed to form a path that trailed into the distance. "It must be that way!"

28

SEEING RED

Uma struggled to keep up with El Jefe. His gelled hair glistened with multi-coloured sparkles of reflected light as he followed the line of orange flashes. It was as though he'd forgotten Uma was there.

She looked around. From the outside, Izcal wasn't much bigger than Fir Lodge. So how could the temple be this huge inside? Uma remembered how hot her hands had felt inside the tent, and how they'd burned when she touched the temple wall. The white glow was still in her palms, rotating and pulsating in a swirling spiral. There was something magical about Izcal – that was for sure.

The rope around her waist pulled tight and El Jefe dragged her forward.

"Come on," he shouted. "Keep up!"

"Wait." Uma stood her ground. She looked at the

lights. Orange wasn't the only colour that was making a path of light. A green trail led to the left. Red flares veered off to the right. "Why orange?" she said. "Why not green? Or red? We have all the colours of the rainbow here."

El Jefe looked up. "You know, the Incas reckoned rainbows were some kind of bridge between spiritual realms. If you believe all that stuff."

Professor Harris had said the same thing.

El Jefe walked up to Uma. "So have you seen something? Harris said your mother could see things."

Uma sat down. "Give me a minute." She couldn't see, not like Mum. But the way El Jefe had run off after the orange lights reminded her of something. Yes … it was like the time Imp had tried to teach her levitation and she'd got distracted by the idea of flying. El Jefe wanted to find Iticanga but had got carried away in the idea of all the money he would make. What had Imp said? "Focus," she muttered to herself. "Focus."

Imp climbed up Uma's sleeve and sat on her shoulder. "So you do listen to me sometimes!"

Uma gazed at the floor. Yes, sometimes. Not often enough.

"Let me do something," Imp said. "You know, teamwork!"

Uma stared at the lights that burst around the cavern. Blue? Red? Green? A rainbow between the realms? What did that mean?

"Maybe," Imp said, "it would help to look at the

bigger picture."

Uma teased a strand of hair and slipped it between her lips. The bigger picture? She looked around. Where did the coloured lights come from? Not from the ground, or the ceiling. They seemed to randomly pop out of the dark. Yes – what had Edgar said? Something about black absorbing all colours. "I have an idea." Uma sat on her knees.

"What are you doing?" El Jefe said.

She trailed her fingers over the rough surface of the stony ground. The rock was solid but not quite smooth. "Here."

"You know the way?" El Jefe stepped closer.

"We need to make a rainbow," Uma said. She wasn't sure her idea would work. She knew prisms diffused light, but she needed to pull light back together. "Is there any water left?"

El Jefe pulled a canister out of his backpack and handed it over. Uma made a puddle in the shallow indentation. The wet patch had to be outside the shield. "Let's move away from the water."

The puddle began to vibrate as soon as it was away from the shield's protection. Rays of red light shot into the water like metal shavings pulled towards a magnet. As soon as they landed, the rays reflected up in a tower of red. Uma watched. One by one the other colours were drawn into the puddle then reflected back: red, orange, yellow, green, blue and indigo, one shade short of a rainbow.

Finally, a band of purple shot into the puddle, and a multi-coloured cloud of smoke puffed up. The cloud writhed and twisted, moulding into a distinctive shape.

"What's THAT?" Imp shouted from Uma's pocket.

She tugged El Jefe's sleeve but he was already staring slack-jawed at the hazy, light-filled dragon's head on the ground.

"Is it real?" Uma said. It didn't look real. Not like it could bite, or attack, or anything.

"Chuichu," El Jefe said. "The Inca's rainbow god. Freaky."

The dragon's mouth opened and purple light burst out. It blended with the multi-coloured tower and began to spin, shooting up, twisting into an arc and curving down towards the floor. A rainbow!

"Pretty," Imp said, smiling.

El Jefe grabbed Uma's shoulder and pointed. "What have you done?"

Uma looked up. The edges of the protective shield were undulating, spreading out and thinning. A green thread travelled through the shield and whizzed past Uma's face. She held up her hands and shot a beam out of her palms. But instead of strengthening the shield, the light tore small holes in the roof. Flecks of burning white dropped like volcanic ash. The shield was coming apart!

Now what?

Uma didn't know what to do. She watched as the rainbow completed its arc and hit the ground. Another cloud billowed and formed a second dragonhead. As its mouth opened, a breath of bright, white light spewed out tracing a line over the rainbow, swallowing up the colours and replacing them with a swirling arc of clear white that whirled up from the ground at their feet.

Was this the Vortex?

El Jefe's face broke into a smile. "The portico!" He turned to Uma. "Through here. Let's go."

White heat steamed off the arc. It looked smouldering-iron hot. "Is it safe?" Uma said.

"Sure." El Jefe gripped her shoulder. "Your parents got through, so why shouldn't we?"

As they got closer, Uma's skin prickled with sweat. Professor Harris had said anything could happen and she was pretty sure 'anything' included getting microwaved to a crisp.

"Let's be quick." El Jefe took her arm and pulled Uma along. Her face and hair glowed in the white haze. Was it some type of radiation? Or whatever had aged Professor Harris? She pulled back but felt El Jefe's grip tighten.

Imp held out his arms. "Incredible."

The rays soaked into Uma's skin and her palms burned hot. They stepped through to the other side and the portico immediately disappeared into the ground. Uma screwed up her eyes and blinked.

All she could see was red.

As though they'd walked into a mist of glittering crimson.

Uma could feel the ground but her feet were hidden

by vapour. It was like standing in a hall of mirrors and not knowing where the reflection starts or ends.

"Harris called this Pachacuti's Cloud," El Jefe said. "He said they walked for a while and then the mist lifted." He didn't sound too sure. "We should be able to see something."

Uma was too scared to move. In case she hit a wall. Or fell down a pit. Nothing seemed solid. "Any ideas?" she said to Imp.

"You talking to me?" El Jefe said. "Or yourself again?"

Uma pushed a hand into the red fog. It felt soft and thick like velvet. "Just thinking out loud."

Imp stood on Uma's shoulder. "What about if you tried *seeing through* the mist?" he said.

"Yes." That would give her an advantage and an opportunity to get away.

El Jefe bumped into Uma as he sidled over. "Is it dangerous to turn on my flashlight?"

"Best not. Remember what happened last time. Anyway, I have an idea." Uma's hand shook as she pulled Edgar's penknife out of her pocket. "It's a way to make the mist thin out, but I need your help."

She heard El Jefe shuffle across the stony ground. "What do I do?" he said.

First of all, she needed to distract him. "It's something Mum used to do, that involves going into a deep meditative state. Aunt Calista taught me," Uma lied. She took a deep breath and explained. "I'm going to chant OM for a while and then go silent. When I'm done, I'll know how to get through the mist." Uma's throat felt dry and scratchy. She hoped El Jefe would fall for her plan.

"And that'll work?" He didn't sound sure.

"It's all I can think of right now," Uma said. "And Mum used this technique. I mean if we walk into the mist blind we might fall down a crevice, or something."

"Yeah, yeah, ok." El Jefe pulled the cord around Uma's waist. "Just remember you can't get away. So are you gonna sit down?"

Uma hadn't thought of that but, yes, it would be even better. "Cross-legged on the floor. And it might take a few minutes for this to work."

Uma felt a pull on the rope around her waist as she settled on the ground. The tightness forced El Jefe to sit down next to her, just as Uma had hoped. "OK, here goes," she said. "OOOOOMMMMMM, OOOOOMMMMMM, OOOOOMMMMMM." Her chant started off faint and shaky but got louder and sharper as she kept going.

"Can you see yet?" Imp said after a few seconds.

Uma shook her head.

"OK." Imp sat on her shoulder. "Try imagining your head is filled with clear water. Move that image into your eyes, and then open them while holding onto that feeling of clarity. Does that make sense?"

Uma didn't think so. But she had to try. She closed her eyes and focused on the sound of her voice and the feel of the rough cord around her waist. El Jefe had no way to see through the mist, so was completely helpless.

This was her best, maybe only, chance of escape. But if she messed up then he wouldn't trust her again and she would probably never get away.

"Stay calm," Imp said. "Remember the light in your hands, how you made that protective shield. You can do this, Uma."

El Jefe moved closer. "How's it going?"

Uma gave an exaggerated sigh. "I was just getting into the zone, and now I have to start again. Please just let me focus."

"OK, OK," he said.

Uma breathed in deeply through her nose and cupped her hands over her eyes. "OOOOOMMMMMM, OOOOOMMMMMM, OOOOOMMMMMM."

The heat from her palms seeped into her head. She felt calm. The picture of a bright, pristine crystal came to mind. She imagined a small piece break off and drop into a glimmering, transparent pool of light. When Uma looked up, she still saw the red mist, but it was sheer, like a fine veil.

"You've done it, haven't you?" Imp said.

Uma nodded and stopped chanting. Trying to move slow as a ninja, Uma held the rope still around her waist and sliced it with Edgar's knife. The rope came apart. Uma left the cord on the floor, sprang up and ran.

"WHAT?" El Jefe jumped to his feet. "HOW DID YOU ... ?"

She kept running. Through the mist Uma saw rock walls bordering the cavern, but no passages. There was nowhere to go. El Jefe ran in her direction.

"He can hear your footsteps!" Imp said.

Uma stopped. El Jefe stood still, head tilted to one side as he listened for movement. His eyes were blank and sightless.

Uma had a proper look around. Only a few metres away she saw a wide bank of narrow steps, the kind she'd seen in pictures of Inca pyramids. The thick, writhing torsos of snakes were etched into the rock walls next to steps that lead down a steep incline. Uma lifted a foot and took a slow, silent step backwards. El Jefe gazed blankly into the mist. He unzipped his jacket. She took another step, edging away.

Then Uma saw the gun.

El Jefe pointed the weapon in her direction but down towards her feet. Like a policeman entering a dark building, he moved his outstretched arms from side to side.

Uma moved back.

El Jefe fired shots into the mist. Low shots aimed at her legs.

She ran toward the stairs.

El Jefe followed behind. "I don't want to hurt you, Uma, but you're making this real hard." He fired two more shots. Uma heard a loud crack as a bullet hit the ground by her feet. She didn't hear the second round. A red-hot pain blasted her leg and tore open her calf. Thick, warm blood trickled down her leg, and Uma fell to the floor.

Imp jumped off her shoulder and pushed a small piece of fabric into Uma's hands. "Use my jacket to put pressure on the wound." She groaned as Imp ran off.

"This didn't need to happen." El Jefe edged closer, moving slowly through the mist. He held one hand out, feeling for obstacles, like someone playing Blind Man's Bluff.

Uma watched Imp race up El Jefe's leg, jump onto his arm and scurry down the gun. What was he doing? She tried to sit up without making noise. But as soon as she moved, El Jefe spun round. He pointed the weapon in her direction. Imp was hanging head first over the barrel of the gun. He squirmed and twisted, doing who knew what. Uma felt sick. If El Jefe fired the gun, Imp would die.

El Jefe advanced through the mist, getting closer. Uma clenched her jaw to stop herself from crying out in pain and dragged herself upright. It would be impossible to move without making noise, but her only option was to get to the steps as fast as possible – and hope El Jefe wouldn't shoot. Or that, next time, he would miss.

Uma hobbled, hauling her injured leg along the ground. She heard a click as El Jefe went to fire another shot. He stopped for a second. "What the - ?"

Still running, Uma turned to look. El Jefe tapped the gun and cursed under his breath.

"I've jammed the barrel," Imp said, landing on Uma's shoulder. "Let's get away, quick."

Uma was close to the stairs now. El Jefe ran blindly

in her direction.

She hesitated. The steps were steep, each one narrower than a small adult foot. As Uma took her first step down, stone fragments crumbled and broke off in small cascades that tumbled into the unseen depths. The debris fell a long time before Uma heard it hit bottom. She turned sideways and carefully made her way down.

El Jefe was still running, flashing his gun from side to side, desperate to catch up.

He didn't see the steps and plunged straight down, rolling onto his side, arms flailing as he tried to catch his balance.

The crumbling stone couldn't take El Jefe's weight. It gave way and he slithered down. As he rocketed past Uma, his leg caught her in the back and she pitched forward. Shoulders crashing on steps, elbows smashing, she rolled behind El Jefe.

Uma wrapped her arms around her head and waited to hit bottom.

29

LAKE ITICANGA

Uma couldn't move her legs.

Sharp rock fragments pressed into her cheek and everything hurt. Everything except her limbs, anyway. Uma slowly moved her neck and lifted her head off the floor. She saw El Jefe. His eyes were closed, his face stained with blood that oozed from a criss-cross of deep scratches. Was he dead?

Uma pulled herself onto her elbows and grappled closer, dragging heavy, lifeless legs. El Jefe lay spread-eagled at the foot of the steps, his limbs twisted into strange, painful-looking contortions. What if neither of them could walk? How would they get out? How would they get anywhere?

Uma tried to sit but it hurt. She tried wriggling onto one side but couldn't turn the dead weight of her legs. Lifting an arm off the ground, she saw that her hand was swollen, red and angry from the fall. She wriggled her fingers but only two moved. Shock must be blocking the pain, but that would wear off soon enough. Uma reached into her jacket for Edgar's army knife. It was gone. She lay back and felt inside her empty pockets. Imp was gone too.

"What are you doing?" El Jefe rasped.

Uma turned slowly to face him. "Trying to find a tissue," she lied.

El Jefe gave a nasty but triumphant grin. "Yeah, well, we've arrived. Look."

Uma looked around and followed his weak gaze. They were in a glistening underground grotto. And a few metres away lay a vast and gleaming stretch of golden water. It was flat as a mirror and shimmered far into the distance. Lake Iticanga.

El Jefe grabbed a trouser leg with his good arm and clumsily untangled his limbs. "Nothing's broken," he said. "That was lucky."

Uma dropped back to the stony ground. "I can't move my legs."

El Jefe half stood. He leaned over and grabbed the frayed rope that hung from Uma's waist. "Where's the knife?" He pulled at the rope, crushing fresh bruises. Uma groaned.

"Lost," she said.

El Jefe patted down Uma's pockets. "Right." He smiled. "Seeing as how you can't walk, guess you won't be running off any time soon." He carefully slipped the backpack over his injured, oozing arm. "Don't go anywhere," he said with a dry laugh. "You're my ride home!"

Uma watched El Jefe stagger to the lake's edge. This was her chance to get away, but she was totally helpless.

"Imp!" Uma pulled herself onto her elbows and tried moving her feet. Nothing. Wasn't this what happened to people with broken backs? She looked at the steps towering above. Then down towards the lake. Imp was lying face down and immobile at the water's edge.

El Jefe let out a hoot of strangled laughter. He stood waist high in the lake, bathing his arms, torso, face and head. Iticanga wasn't made of water at all. It was a pool of shimmering, golden light. Uma scanned its surface into the horizon, looking for signs of danger. Where was the Vortex?

El Jefe turned to Uma and waved like a kid on a summer's beach. "You should come in!" he said, knowing she could barely move.

Uma squinted. Did she have concussion? Or was she losing her mind? Every scratch on El Jefe's face had disappeared.

He rolled up his sleeves and held out his arms. "Do you see?" The burns had gone, replaced by fresh, new skin.

Uma's eyes filled with tears. Professor Harris had said Iticanga was a healing lake but this was way more than anything she'd imagined. Of course Mum and Dad had wanted to come. And if they'd survived, they would have made sure everyone could use the lake's energy. She looked across at Imp and, ignoring the sharp pain in her chest, pushed herself onto her elbows. Taking quick, shallow breaths Uma inched towards him.

El Jefe trailed out of the lake, smiling. He walked to his backpack, pulled out another cord and tied it first round his waist then Uma's. Her eyes watered as he tightened the rope and secured it with a reef knot.

"Your turn." He hauled her up and waded into the lake. Uma wanted to tell him to wait. She wanted to reach Imp but had no way to explain.

Uma looked over El Jefe's shoulder. Imp still hadn't moved and she couldn't tell whether or not he was breathing. He never stayed still for more than thirty seconds at a time. Not ever.

El Jefe lowered Uma into Iticanga. It felt fizzy, like sherbet air. Warm waves rolled over her legs and she felt a pulse of energy surge through her legs and up her spine. Pushing away from El Jefe, Uma dropped into the lake and tried to stand. Her legs worked ... she could walk.

"Follow me." El Jefe tugged the rope impatiently and dragged Uma to the edge of the lake. "I'll collect some of the waters, then we can leave. For now."

For now. Yes. Of course. El Jefe would need her to get in and out of Izcal. And once he had everything he wanted? What then? Somehow she had to get away. But first, she had to help Imp.

Uma bent down and scooped golden light into her

hands then threw it hard in Imp's direction.

"Stop messing about." El Jefe pulled the rope, dragging Uma to where his bag lay. Imp still didn't move.

El Jefe took two clear plastic canisters out of his bag and towed Uma back to the lake. She stumbled along, looking over her shoulder at Imp's motionless figure.

El Jefe dipped the first canister into the waters and held it up. "Too weak."

The lake was a deep, shimmering gold, but the light in the canister was faint, almost transparent.

El Jefe plunged the second canister deep down. "Better," he said, examining the slightly darker fluid. "But not good enough. We need to head further out, where the waters are deeper." He scanned the shimmering surface then pointed. "There!"

Uma saw a slight rippling at the centre of the lake where the light bubbled a deeper shade of gold.

"That's what we need!" El Jefe said. "The Vortex!"

THE VORTEX

"Stop gawping and let's go!" El Jefe waded into the lake.

The rope pressed hard against Uma's waist as she followed, diving into the strange, iridescent fog. "Professor Harris says the Vortex is dangerous. Mum and Dad were killed here."

El Jefe kept going. "He never told me that."

Uma struggled to catch up. "Well, something killed my parents."

"Harris told me they drowned." El Jefe pushed away in a strong breaststroke.

Uma wished he would stop or slow down. "You mean they drowned in light?"

El Jefe wasn't listening.

"Wait!" Uma said. "I can't swim as fast as you!"

"You know, I liked you better when your legs didn't

work." El Jefe kept going.

Uma hung back. She heard a soft voice somewhere close by and spun round.

"Help! Help!"

It was Imp, but WHERE?

Uma checked the shoreline. Nothing.

She checked the lake. And there, bobbing up and down was the top of Imp's head. He was maybe swimming, maybe drowning.

Uma felt the cord tighten around her waist as El Jefe ploughed on. "What's the hold-up?"

"I've got cramp." Uma grabbed the back of her leg and twisted her face into what was supposed to be a look of pain.

"Cramp? You can't get cramp in here." El Jefe swam up. "Do you think I'm stupid?"

Uma let herself drift towards the shoreline, closer to Imp. She quickly looked back. He was almost close enough, if she could just reach out.

She felt a sharp pain in her head as El Jefe yanked her hair. He pulled Uma's face close to his and she made out a small trail of spittle at the side of his mouth.

El Jefe tugged and wrenched Uma's neck, making her eyes water. "I've hurt a ton of people to get this far and no snotty-nosed kid's going to stop me now! Get it?"

Uma couldn't move her head to nod. She leaned away from El Jefe, still stretching an arm out behind her back. "You're going to get us killed," she said. "The Vortex is dangerous!"

El Jefe stared at Uma with contempt. "No. *I'm* dangerous," he said. "This is my chance – money, respect, power. That's all that matters in this world."

Even though her shoulder ached, Uma held out her arm like a human life raft. She prayed Imp could grab it. "Don't people matter? Everyone you hurt to find Professor Harris?"

El Jefe snorted and loosened the grip on Uma's hair. "I'm in too deep. Borrowed money from loan sharks and all kinds. Let's GO."

Uma rubbed the side of her head. She felt a tug on her sleeve and quickly looked round. Imp was scrambling up her arm, clutching Edgar's knife.

"I thought it would come in useful," he said, collapsing into the crook of Uma's neck.

"Thank you." She gave his tiny arm a squeeze. "I'm so glad you're ok."

"Nearly there!" Light sprayed off El Jefe's chest as he pushed through the waters. "I need to find some way to pipe this stuff out." He was talking to himself, eyes shining gold from the pool's reflected light. "Next to me, the oil men are gonna look like down-and-outs."

A turbulent swell spilled out of the Vortex and Uma felt waves build and push into her chest. The pulsating was getting stronger but El Jefe didn't notice.

"Look at this stuff!" He swished his hand through the golden mist. "Have you ever seen anything like it? Just waiting to be bottled up and sold on."

Uma struggled against the current. The rope

squeezed tight around her waist.

"Soon, right?" Imp clung to a strand of Uma's hair.

She clutched the knife and watched El Jefe approach the Vortex.

Yes. Now.

Uma held the rope tight and slashed. It frayed. She sliced again and again.

El Jefe didn't look back. "Nearly there!"

Uma pulled the knife hard across the rope, but as soon as the threads severed they re-joined, intact and strong.

"You need to hold the rope out of the water," Imp said. "The lake is fixing the broken strands."

"Here!" El Jefe lifted a canister high over his head. "This'll be where we find the purest light."

Imp pulled Uma's hair. "Look!"

She put down the knife while El Jefe approached the rocking waves of the Vortex. As he edged forward, a massive, golden surge spilled up to form a thick barrier of golden light. In its centre was a golden sun with rays snaking from its centre. Just like on the temple wall and Harris' letter.

"What?!" El Jefe pushed forward and immersed his hand through the swirling wall. He screamed and pulled back. His hand was burnt and blistered. Face twisted in pain, El Jefe thrust his arm into the lake and black vapours rose out of the waters.

Uma saw something shimmer behind the golden wall. As though bands of light were tearing, coming apart then reconnecting to form an outline. Like had happened with the dragonheads. El Jefe swam towards Uma and they watched in awe.

A human silhouette appeared before their eyes. No – two human silhouettes. A man and woman stood on the water's surface either side of the golden sun. Patches of light thickened and the outlines slowly filled with detail. Eyes, noses, mouths.

Uma's breath wedged in a hard lump at the centre of her chest. "MUM? DAD?" She raced up to the wall of light.

"No!" Mum took a step forward. "Stay away! It's dangerous." She lifted a hand as though she wanted to reach out and touch Uma. "We knew you'd come," she said in a whisper, "but didn't think it would be so soon."

Uma's breath came in tight, ragged whispers. "You're alive?" she said.

Dad shook his head. "No. Not alive."

Uma didn't understand. El Jefe grabbed her shoulder and laughed. "Right! So you're what?" he said. "Spooky-wooky ghosts?" His voice was child-like and mocking.

Mum and Dad thinned and dispersed into clouds of smoke.

"No," Uma shouted. "Please don't go!"

She watched the golden light reform as Mum and Dad.

"Nothing really dies," Dad said. He turned to Uma, his eyes soft and sad. "It's just, nothing stays the same. Everything is always changing."

Uma understood the look in Dad's eyes. *Nothing stays the same.* She'd changed since he'd last seen her. The four-year old Uma had gone. Died, in a way. Just like Mum and Dad had died in their way.

Dad turned to El Jefe. "There's no way out of the Vortex."

Uma knew that, but still wanted Mum and Dad to come home. *Why* couldn't they come home?

El Jefe pulled the rope out of the water and waved it in the air. "You know why I'm here," he said. "And in case you missed the fact, Uma and I are kind of attached. You know, like inseparable."

Mum and Dad turned to El Jefe, calm and impassive. "We see that," Dad said.

"Good. Just so things are real clear ..." El Jefe tugged the rope and pulled Uma forward. "Unless you want me, I mean *us*, to come in there," he said, "you better bring some of that Vortex light out. Get my drift?"

Uma lunged forward. "I want to stay here. Please!" She wanted to be with Mum and Dad – even if they only were a kind of strange hologram.

"Stop her!" Dad said.

El Jefe's fingers gripped Uma's arm. "Not so fast," he said with a smirk. "That's not how this is going to play out."

Uma covered her eyes. "But I don't want things to change!" She looked up. Stupid. Things had changed a long time ago.

Mum took a step forward. "This is our home now,"

she said. "Yours is with Aunt Calista. Maybe come back one day, when you're older. In the meantime, just remember there is one thing that never changes." Mum smiled. "Our energy is with you all the time, wherever you go, even when you can't see us. We're connected. Do you understand? Always and every second."

Uma fought back tears and stared at Mum. And Dad. Holding onto every detail of the moment, to never forget.

El Jefe pushed Uma to the side. "This is all very touching," he said, "but let's move it along. You might have forever, but I sure don't."

Mum looked at Dad and gave a small nod.

"Wait there," Dad said. "I'll bring you the most powerful healing light there is."

"Yeah." El Jefe grabbed Uma's hair and pulled her close. "Just don't try anything funny. Or baby girl gets it."

31

DROWNING NOT WAVING

Uma watched Dad disappear in a flicker of light. She felt a scuffle on her shoulder.

"Awesome," Imp whispered, wiping orange tears from his eyes.

Mum held a hand over her mouth. "*Bartholomew?*"

"What?" El Jefe pulled out his gun. "WHERE?"

Uma twisted away from El Jefe. Did Mum mean Imp? She lifted him off her shoulder. "You can see him?" she said.

"What's going on?" El Jefe said. "Harris told me about Bartholomew but in all these years no one ever heard of him, or saw him. Tell me!" El Jefe uselessly held up his weapon.

Ignoring El Jefe, Mum gave a knowing smile. "He looks like those creatures in my old picture books," she said.

Eyes flitting nervously from side to side, El Jefe lowered the gun and gripped Uma's shoulder. "Who's she talking about?"

It was Uma's chance to smirk. "The same person I talk to when you think I'm talking to myself."

"Bartholomew's an imaginary friend?" El Jefe spat.

"Not really imaginary." Uma turned to Mum. "Please explain."

Mum nodded. "Did Aunt Calista tell you what happened to my powers after your grandfather died?"

Uma slipped Imp back onto her shoulder. She had so many questions. "Aunt Calista said you forgot it all."

Mum nodded. "And I knew the same would happen to you … if we didn't make it back for some reason." She turned away for a second. "Before leaving, I created a sort of energy void inside a knot in Blankie … a place for the energy-bending part of yourself to go. Things only become material when they have a name, so I called it Bartholomew." She grinned. "You were only four so it makes sense that you'd fill the void with a sprite-like creature! He looks fun. Hello, Bartholomew!"

Imp stood tall on Uma's shoulder. "She calls me Imp," he said. "But Bartholomew has more gravitas. I like it better."

"Enough, already! Is this a trick?" El Jefe pushed Uma forwards, up towards the Vortex.

At that moment, Dad reappeared holding a roughly hewn silver pot. A cloud of golden light billowed from its neck. "Here," Dad said, "but you need to come closer."

El Jefe relaxed and his eyes glistened.

"Wait! I have something for Uma." From behind the wall, Mum held out a small, golden ball of light. "A keepsake," she said. The ball flew out of her hand. It shot through the centre of the sun in the wall of light. When it came out the other side it had turned into a flat disk.

El Jefe grabbed it before Uma could reach. "Nice." He slipped the disk into the front pouch of his backpack.

"It's mine!" Uma lunged for the bag.

El Jefe pushed an arm hard into her chest and Uma stumbled back. "It's gold," he said. "Now give me what I need."

Dad held out the silver pot and El Jefe approached.

Uma looked at Mum for guidance. What now?

Mum gave a calm smile and nodded. Uma turned her head away. It was time.

Imp scrambled down Uma's arm and into the lake. He tugged at the rope and lifted it out of the waters. "Come on, Uma. Let's go, go, go!"

Dad held El Jefe's gaze. "Tell us. Who are you? And where's Professor Harris?"

Uma hurried. This was her only chance. Hoping Dad could distract El Jefe, Uma unsheathed the army knife and sliced at the rope.

"Harris is indisposed," El Jefe said. "Now – you going to hand over that thing, or what?"

Uma kept slashing. If El Jefe turned around and saw, it would all be over.

The rope split. She grabbed the end that was tied to

El Jefe and kept tugging. He had to think she was still attached and keeping up.

El Jefe reached the wall of light and smiled. "So how is this going to work?"

"I'll pass it through, just like Uma's keepsake." Mum closed her eyes and lifted her arms above her head. "Hanpuy!" she shouted. "Hanpuy!" At her command, the sun in the wall of light began spinning, faster and faster. After a few seconds, the wall pulsed forward and engulfed El Jefe.

Uma quickly let go of the rope and pushed back with her legs. She searched for Mum and Dad but they had gone. Back into the Vortex.

El Jefe reappeared, thrown high in a jet of golden light that gushed from the centre of the Vortex. He rose, fell and somersaulted. And as the light climbed, it gradually darkened. The sound of his blood-chilling screams filled the cavern.

Imp clutched Uma tight. She watched as grey silhouettes formed around El Jefe's body. The shadows thickened into dark tendrils that slid around his thrashing limbs. They bound him tight, wrapping him in a black cocoon, like a fly trapped in a spider's web. Gradually, the threads disappeared, merging back into the gold. El Jefe was nothing more than a small black dot on the glowing surface of the golden light fountain. Uma covered her ears. Whatever was happening, she could still make out his desperate cries. Slowly, the dot sank into the lake.

"We should go," Imp said.

"I guess." Uma swam away. She looked over her shoulder just as the cocoon disappeared into the centre of the Vortex. A lump jammed in Uma's throat. She was leaving Mum and Dad – but what else could she do?

Then she saw El Jefe's backpack floating in the lake. She lashed out and swam towards the Vortex.

"No!" Imp said. "Wrong way!"

Ignoring Imp's shouts, Uma pushed against the current and stretched out to grab the bobbing bag. It was just out of reach.

"Please!" Imp tugged her hair. "Let's get out of here!"

At that moment, another, bigger wave emerged from the Vortex, gradually building and gathering force.

Imp clung to Uma's collar. "Let's go!"

Uma paddled faster, up to El Jefe's backpack. She pushed her hand into the front pocket and grabbed the gold disk. "I've got it!" she said.

A huge swell of water rose in front of Uma's face. She turned, kicking her legs, arms flailing. But it was too late. The wave picked Uma up and carried her along as though she were driftwood. Muscles tearing, breath heavy, Uma looked up. A golden tower of light soared over her head, high as a mushroom cloud and more powerful than anything she had ever seen. The surge was going to sweep her away and there was nothing she could do.

Imp tugged her ear. "Uma, you've got to try."

He was right. She raised her hands over her head,

closed her eyes and drove white heat out of her palms. The heat projected up and collided with a shower of light that dropped towards them like an avalanche. A gold flash exploded, burning Uma's eyes and face; her hands were forced back by an enormous, crushing weight.

"You can do it," Imp said. "Keep going."

Uma strained as long as she could. Her arms trembled, but it was too much. Exhausted, her hands dropped and Uma shot backwards. She pelted through the air faster and faster, out of control like a rocket travelling beyond the speed of light. It was impossible to see, breathe or feel.

"Hold on, Imp." Uma shut her eyes and waited for the end.

32

HOMEWARD

Uma stirred. It was bright and her head was achy. Did that mean she was alive? That she'd made it out? She opened her eyes and a sharp, blinding pain shot through her skull. Uma saw winding roots, leaves and the temple's ancient stonework - enough to know she'd definitely got out of Izcal. She closed her eyes and drifted into unconsciousness.

Hours later, Uma felt a soft tickle flutter around her ear, sending goose bumps down her neck and arms. She pulled open her lids, and sunlight made her eyes prickle and tear.

"Hello-o-o! You're leaking all over me!"

"Imp! It's you!" Uma lifted her head to see Imp standing on her chest, hand on hip.

He grinned. "Of course. Who else would it be?"

Uma sat and scooped him up. "We made it out," she said.

"Yes. And the good news is that you're not 120!"

Uma looked closely at her hands. "Yes. I'm still me." She didn't know why Professor Harris had aged and she hadn't, but was grateful.

"El Jefe's gone," Imp said.

Uma nodded. So were Mum and Dad but she wasn't ready to think about that. She reached into her pocket. The golden disc was there, safe – her reminder of what had happened. "Thanks, Imp," she said. "I couldn't have done it without you."

"Yes, well," Imp stared at his feet and shuffled from side to side. "I, well ... you're right. And you owe me three jellybeans." He grinned. "To replace the ones I stuffed down the barrel of El Jefe's gun."

It hurt to laugh, but Uma couldn't help it.

She sniffed. "What's that terrible smell?"

The stink was pongy, twiggy, and vaguely familiar. Listening carefully, she could just make out the sound of voices. "Do you hear that?" she whispered.

Imp clambered up Uma's arm and onto her shoulder. He stared her down, one eyebrow raised. "Can I hear that? That racket's been driving me mad the whole time you've been conked out. It's Aunt Calista, Edgar, Steve and Professor Harris."

"What about Barrel and Stick?"

Imp shook his head. "Nope."

Uma hesitated. "Because if they're still here then I

should probably stay hidden for now." She wasn't sure. "I mean, the element of surprise and all that … you haven't heard Barrel and Stick at all?"

"Not a peep. But that smell is unmistakable, don't you think?" Imp said.

He was right. Uma crept along the side of the temple and peeked round the wall edge. Aunt Calista, Edgar, Steve and Professor Harris were sitting round the campfire. A small pot of Aunt Calista's herbal tea simmered, spreading its noxious odour into the surrounding rainforest. There was no sight of El Jefe's henchmen and one of the cars was gone.

Uma's head ached and she just wanted to go home. So much had happened, it would take a while to figure it all out. She walked towards the campfire. "Aunt Calista?"

Her aunt turned and jumped to her feet. "Thank goodness!" She rushed over and threw her arms around Uma. Professor Harris and Steve stood up, watching and waiting.

Aunt Calista held Uma at arm's length and stared into her face. "How are you? Do you want some of my tea? It worked wonders on Edgar."

Edgar pulled a face. He looked a little green and Uma was sure the nasty herbs were responsible.

"I feel fine," she said, even though a sharp ache throbbed at the base of her skull. "None for me thanks."

Steve came over and gave her arm a squeeze. "Glad to have you back, mate." His face was tight and pinched. "After seeing you walk through that wall, I knew you'd be alright."

Professor Harris moved a cushion so Uma could sit. "Glad to see you're looking fresh as ever." He pointed first at her smooth skin, then his wrinkles and gave Uma a wink. He patted her arm.

Uma sat down. "So where are Barrel and Stick?"

Aunt Calista laughed. "Professor Harris took care of them – single-handedly."

"Yeah," Steve said. "We all have something to learn from that guy. No muscle no guns, he sent those two thugs running for the hills just with the power of his imagination."

Edgar laughed. "It was totally awesome!"

The Professor took a sip of tea and his face twisted in disgust. "Mm," he said, "fear is one of life's greatest weapons, I've learned that much. Just had to embellish enough tales of death, torture and "hoocha" energy – and off they went in a puff of diesel fumes."

Aunt Calista stoked the fire. "Yeah. They took El Jefe's 4x4, so we'll have to trek back, and although the Professor is fitter than he was, well, it'll take a while."

Uma unzipped her backpack and pulled out the key to Barrel and Stick's car. "Or not," she said.

"Is this for their car?" Aunt Calista grabbed the key. "Let's get packing!"

Professor Harris got to his feet. "Do you think we might stop at the Nazca lines on the way? We could take one of the flights over the glyphs."

"Flights?" Humming nervously, Aunt Calista headed

to the car. "I've heard Machu Picchu's amazing."

Steve squatted next to Uma. "So, El Jefe … ? Where is he? I mean, any chance he's going to get out?"

Uma shook her head. "No chance," she said. "None at all."

"Alright." Steve squeezed her shoulder. "Sorry to bring it up. Here," he held out his hand, "let's get you home. You can tell us everything on the way. If you like."

Uma settled into the car between Professor Harris and Edgar. She stared at the glowing, peaceful temple. The stonework gave no hint as to the force of the healing and destructive powers inside. Professor Harris might have made up the thing about Izcal being a funerary monument but to Uma it was exactly that – the place Mum and Dad had died, their tomb. One day, she'd be back, that much Uma knew. When she was older, like Mum had said. Once she really knew some energy bending.

Aunt Calista put a hand on Uma's knee. "Are you ready?"

Uma nodded.

Steve started up the engine and they set off on the long drive back to Lima.

"You know," Aunt Calista said, "seeing the whole energy bending thing in action after all this time, it's given me loads of ideas for new inventions. I'm taking a whole new approach – you're going to be amazed!"

Imp climbed from Uma's pocket up to her shoulder. "Have you noticed how quiet I've been? The way I haven't chipped in, not even once?" He settled into the crook of her neck. "Well, you should know that I'm not sure how long I can keep that up."

Visit Uma and Imp's
blog at

WWW.IMPPRINTBOOKS.COM

to read more about
their lives and
adventures.